Reconstructing Christmas

an anthology

Reconstructing Christmas: an anthology by various authors

Published by SJ Blasko
Cover & formatting by SJ Blasko
Title page image by Jana Vrbíková (https://www.fler.cz/violka-atelier)

All work used with permission.
ISBN: 978-1-951882-05-1

for our younger selves

and anyone else

who needs to know that they are loved

(especially by their God)

More from the authors:

An Offer of Grace series by Chloe Flanagan

She Speaks: Twenty Years of Silence by Joya Polk

The *Daughter of Magic* trilogy by Karen Eisenbrey

The Gospel According to St. Rage by Karen Eisenbrey

Buscando Home series by Allison K. García

Vivir el Dream by Allison K. García

Honeysuckle by Meagan Ruby Wagner

The Morning After by Raelee May Carpenter

Liberation Song by Raelee May Carpenter

Kings and Shepherds by Raelee May Carpenter

The Lincoln High Project by Raelee May Carpenter

the kin-dom in the rubble by Avery Smith

TREE by SJ Blasko

Losing the Stars by SJ Blasko

Midnight Comes by SJ Blasko

the flowers need love to grow too by SJ Blasko

Balancing Act by Johanna E. H.

Cary and John by Neil Ellis Orts

Watch and Pray by Neil Ellis Orts

"In His strength, I will dare and dare and dare until I die."

—*Joan of Arc*

Table of Contents

The Human Jesus; the Outsider Jesus
by Chloe S. Flanagan

I give you a new commandment, that you love one another. Just as I have loved you, you also should love one another. By this everyone will know that you are my disciples, if you have love for one another."

John 13:34-35 (NRSV)

One thing I love about the faith journey is how a perception and understanding of Jesus can change over the years, even though he stays the same. He simply reveals Himself by layers.

The Jesus I met when I was a child was the powerful Jesus. Through Sunday school and church, I learned about the mighty Son of God, who walked on water, calmed storms, and raised the dead.

Then, just before adolescence, I met the benevolent Jesus, and learned that I could have a relationship with him. At first, I couldn't imagine why the powerful Jesus would trouble himself over someone like me, but I grew to learn that his power and benevolence are inextricably linked. His love is for everyone, I learned, including me.

But it wasn't until I was a young adult that I began to meet human Jesus. That's also when I met Barrington Bunny.

Barrington is the title character in a short story by Martin Bell from his collection of Gospel retellings, *The Way of the Wolf*[1]. Barrington is a lone rabbit hopping through the forest one cold Christmas Eve. He searches for companionship among the other animals, but finds that he doesn't belong. He can't climb to visit with the squirrels or swim to be with the beavers. Lonely and despondent, he can only hop back to his home.

On the way, he meets a beautiful silver wolf that reminds him of the unique gifts he's been given as a bunny: his warm fur and ability to hop. He also reminds Barrington that all the animals are his family. Barrington accepts the wolf's wisdom and sets off to give his own gifts to his animal family.

As he is finishing his Christmas errands, he discovers a little lost field mouse shivering in the snow. Barrington covers the mouse with his fur and keeps him safe and warm through the night, rejoicing that he is a soft, warm bunny and that all the animals are his family. The next morning, the

[1] Bell, Martin. *The Way of the Wolf: The Gospel in New Images.* The Random House Publishing Group. Copyright 1968

little mouse's family is so glad to find him, that they don't notice the bunny that has frozen to death protecting their baby mouse from the cold.

Barrington is such a hapless little fellow, that it almost seems irreverent to think of his story as a Christ allegory. Yet, among other things, Barrington captures an important element of the human Jesus: vulnerability. The human Jesus was born in a stable and his family was forced to flee violence at a young age. He was demonized by religious authorities and belittled by his relatives. And as he neared death, he pleaded with his friends to wait with him in his heartache, only to have them abandon him to ridicule and suffering.

This Jesus stands on the outskirts. He is accessible to the outcast, the displaced, the poor, the hungry, the disenfranchised, the refugees, and those of us who have repeatedly been told there is no place in the kingdom of God for us simply because of our identity. This Jesus turns the eyes of the world to the outsider because he was one. And, like the intrepid bunny in Martin Bell's story, he served and saved through his outsider status.

The truly incredible thing is that, just as Jesus elected to share our nature, he invites us to share his as well. He empowers us to love and give of ourselves to others. And I believe the invitation is especially extended to those of us who have experienced the outsider status. He *is* us and we *are* him: the ones in the desert place, serving and loving right where we are, regardless of what the established religion does or doesn't think about it. We have the opportunity to offer grace to a broken world by meeting the world where it is. Our uniqueness and our outsider status is salvation.

This Christmas and all throughout the New Year, I pray we are blessed with the opportunity and will to *be* Jesus to one another, and to seek him in the faces of all people. Amen.

Who Is Christmas?
by Joya Polk

Christmas used to be my favorite time of the year,
And now, like the rest of my life, it's turned into a
shallow pit of depression.
A short fall, really.
And by fall, I mean fail.
A melancholy tale,
One you'd prefer not to hear.
In fact, I'm sure you've stopped reading by now.
That's okay.
The holidays are for MY healing.

Tradition says,
Spend time with your family.
Tradition says,
You better go home and spend time with you
family.

I say,
My family is not healthy for me right now.
I say,
My family is not healthy for me right now.
I say,
My family is not healthy for me right now.

My therapist is the only one who validates me.

The narrative is simple but controversial:
No one believes the child.
No one believes the child who grew up in the
suburbs with picture-perfect Christian parents
who raised you right.
How dare you struggle?
What could possibly be the cause of your
depression?
Certainly not them.
Certainly not Christ.
Certainly not the gifts.
Certainly not the reason for the season.

So why are the holidays not so happy?

Maybe it's because I was so high on the twinkling
lights and 'merry-this' on tights that I thought it
better to be with sweet baby Jesus two days after
his birthday last year.
Simply put,
I'd rather not be home for the holidays.
I'd rather be me for the holidays.
But that's just not possible in the Month of
December.
So I'm just waiting on January.
January:
Ready for the self repair,

Ready for the new beginning,
Ready for leaving another year of trauma behind.

Knitting a Cap for Marina
by Karen Eisenbrey

[Content Warning: brief scene set during a lockdown drill, talk of school shootings]

"What are you working on, Carol Anne? I thought you'd finished that project."

"Hey, Mom." I barely glance up from my needles. Some people can knit without looking, but I'm not that good yet. "I'm almost finished. Just knitting a cap for Marina."

"Pretty yarn." Mom sits next to me on the couch and leans in. "Have I met Marina? She's not in your band, is she?"

"No, but she was on the stage crew for *Anything Goes* last spring." I wish Mom wouldn't watch me work. If she makes me drop a stitch … "You might have met her then. Black hair, stellar eyeliner?" I'm still focused on my knitting but can't help a little smile. That eyeliner.

"Hmm." Mom crosses her arms and gazes up and to the left, as if Marina were hanging from the ceiling like a bat. "No, doesn't ring a bell. So, do you *like* Marina?"

"I like all my friends, Mom."

"You know what I mean."

"Uh-huh." My voice is as bland as can be. "Nothing to see here. Just a beginning knitter trying to finish her Christmas presents before Winter Break."

I taught myself to knit over the summer, from online videos. I made a lumpy practice cap for myself in a nice chocolatey brown. It's ... wearable. When I started knitting for other people, I adopted a practice I'd heard about. I think about the person and knit my prayers for them into the work. I don't know if that was the reason, but I did a better job on a green cap for Barbara's birthday present—not the best choice for a July birthday, but Barbara is very into hats. It's been amazing to watch her rebuild her confidence from absolute zero to delusions of superpowers in less than a year. That's what a band can do for you if the members click. An all-girl band was just what I needed, too. I love playing guitar and I like playing with other people, but sometimes that competitive boy energy can get in the way.

Barbara's cap went over well, so I figured if I kept at it, everyone else could have one for Christmas. Black for Whitney, who uses F-bombs and punk attitude as armor against microaggressions; pink for Storm, the recovering mean girl who uses her queen-bee powers for good; and purple, blue, red, yellow for other friends and family. Marina's the only one left. If she is still my friend.

You would think I'd know, but it's complicated. Because I do like Marina.

Nearly dropped a stitch even without Mom's distractions. I take a breath, slow down, and try to knit in a prayer alongside the fuzzy yarn—charcoal with a strand of silver twisted in. What do I pray for the first girl—the first *person*—I've really wanted to kiss? That she'll notice me, too? That she'll turn gay for me? Those both seem selfish. So I pray for her health. For her safety. For her family, though I know nothing about them. But even the best families can be difficult. That this cap will keep her head warm this winter. I pray that she'll find what she wants in life. With a footnote that I wouldn't mind being part of that.

I've had a secret crush on Marina since the first time she listened to me play my guitar during lunch break. She requested an obscure song that happened to be a favorite of mine. She goes for a goth aesthetic, with her black clothes, dyed-black hair, pale makeup, and dark lipstick (and lest we forget, that eyeliner. Swoon). That would all seem at odds with my colorful, mid-20th-century vintage look, but I admire anyone who can choose a style and rock it. She actually has an incredibly sunny disposition, with dimples to match. I suspect the goth thing is about horrifying the parents, also a choice I can respect. Anyway, we hit it off last spring, working on the musical, and continued to hang out after. Whenever I had my guitar out, I always played her requests first. I thought I was flirting. Maybe I was too subtle.

I wish I could just come out to everybody at once and be done with it. That would make it easier to tell Marina I'm interested. It's a headache keeping track of who knows what. Mom knows, but not Dad yet, because she's convinced he won't take it well. I told Barbara when we were first starting the band. She was cool with it; even invited me to her church. I haven't gone yet, but I might. I miss that part of my old life. Anyway, she already suspected, so maybe it's that obvious and I don't need to worry about it. I haven't told Whitney or Storm outright, but I don't think they'd care.

Maybe Marina has figured it out on her own, like Barbara did. Maybe it's a problem. We're friendly at school, but something's different this year. There's … distance.

I was working up to closing that gap. I was going to drop all the secrecy and invite her to the homecoming dance. Either way, yes or no, would tell me something. But I didn't get the chance. Dylan asked her first and she said yes. That blue-haired emo kid with my dimpled goth girl? OK, not mine, but I'd always assumed he was gay. I understand they made an impression with their Victorian ghost couple routine. I don't think they're together now, though.

So I'm knitting a cap for Marina. It's like her: dark, but sparkly. Frost on a winter night.

The Thursday before break, I put on my forest-green twinset, a vintage skirt with a reindeer print, and the cranberry lipstick Marina complimented that one time. I arrive at school a little early with a tote full of pretty gift bags, and plant myself by Marina's locker. I'll give Storm and Whitney their caps at band practice after school. And I have a striped scarf for Barbara, made from all my leftover yarn. I'll catch other friends in class or at lunch. But I don't want to risk missing Marina.

"Hi, Carol Anne." Marina opens her locker and stashes her backpack. "What's up?"

"Merry Christmas." I hold out the shiny black gift bag with silver tissue frilling out the top.

"Ooh, for me?" She's all wide eyes and dimples as she takes it. Her dark plum lipstick cries out to be kissed. "Can I open it now? Or ... I mean, your gift isn't ready yet. Should I wait?"

"Go ahead and open it," I say. "It doesn't have to be a gift exchange. It's just a little token."

She reaches into the bag and pulls out the cap. "So soft!" She puts it on and instantly becomes even more adorable.

"Oh, good," I say. "It seems to fit you just right. I had to guess what size to make."

"Wait, you *made* this? Carol Anne, you are the most talented person I know. Thank you!"

My face is warmer than it should be, and with my pale skin, the blush absolutely shows. And probably clashes with my hair. "I'm still better with a guitar than knitting needles," I say. "And speaking of, we're playing Saturday—teen band showcase at Salmon Bay Eagles. Just a short set, but …"

"Oh, amazing! I liked what I heard at the homecoming afterparty."

"You were there? I didn't see you." That party was seniors only, and Marina's a junior, so…

"I wasn't *supposed* to be there." Her eyebrows flick up mischievously and my heart flips. "We listened outside the door for a few minutes. But I hope I can—"

We're interrupted by the PA: "This is a lockdown." The bell rings the familiar pattern.

Really? Now? When I was finally getting somewhere and not losing my nerve?

We've had a lot of lockdown drills, but never first thing in the morning. Most people are reasonably calm. I kind of hate that we know what to do. That we *have to* know. I look around when some overly dramatic kid screams. But when I look back, Marina is being swept into a classroom. Before I can catch up, the door closes, and a teacher directs me into a different room. I find a seat and space for my backpack, guitar case, and tote full of gift bags. The teacher shuts and locks the door and turns out the lights. Nobody seems to know what's going on. Whispered rumors fly about someone with a gun, or two people with a gun, or an armed mob. I pull out my phone to text Barbara. Those delusions of superpowers are going to get her into trouble one of these days. I haven't heard back from her by the time the lockdown is lifted.

The rumors are still flying when I get to class. Most of them have settled down to a boy (or a boy and a girl) had a gun on the school grounds but not inside the building. No word about deaths or injuries, but nobody heard any shots. The police came and arrested at least one person. Were they students? No one seems to know. What I do know is, I don't see Barbara all day. When she doesn't appear for band practice, I fear the worst because this band is her life. She would never willingly miss band practice.

I almost forget to give Storm and Whitney their presents. They say nice things and try on their caps, but none of us have much enthusiasm for anything so trivial as Christmas gifts. We run through our four-song set for Saturday, Storm and I doing what we can with Barbara's lead vocals. It's not the same, but we'll make it work if we have to. The show must go on.

In the middle of practice, I get a phone call. I would usually let it go to mail, but it's Barbara's mom. I answer it.

"Carol Anne, I'm so sorry no one called you earlier," she says. "Barbara had … a distressing day and … had to miss school. She just now realized it was band practice day."

"Poor Barbara! She's not sick, is she? Will she have to miss Saturday, too?"

"She's fine now; just tired. She wants to be there on Saturday if she can. She'll let you know."

"OK, tell her we missed her today. 'Bye."

Before school lets out for break, we learn more details. A troubled student brought a gun to school. He didn't shoot or threaten anyone. He didn't even try to get inside, so we were probably never in danger. I'm glad about that and I hope he gets whatever help he needs, but I know who to blame if I've missed my chance with Marina. There were also rumors that Barbara was involved somehow but I'm willing to believe her issue wasn't related.

That said, I have never been so relieved to see anyone as I am when Barbara shows up at the venue on Saturday night. She's subdued and distracted, but she comes alive onstage, throwing everything she has into singing these four songs. I relax into the music and look out over the crowd. They're responding to the music, even joining in on a call-and-response part.

Something glitters in front of the stage. Now I'm glad all the songs are so familiar I could play them in my sleep. Marina came. She's right up front, wearing my cap, eyes on ... me? Maybe us, because we're killing it, but I think she's mostly looking at me.

In no time, our set is done. I come off the stage, put my guitar back in its case, and high-five my bandmates. Around us, the crowd's responding loudly to the next group, a death-metal outfit called Human Blood Rush. I'll never find Marina in this mob scene. But when I turn around, Marina has found me. She screams something I don't catch and throws her arms around me.

I hug her back because of course I do. She whispers in my ear, "Your Christmas present is finally ready." The next thing I know, she's kissing me and I'm totally kissing her back.

I don't usually care for death metal, but Human Blood Rush is my new favorite band. Merry Christmas.

Deconstructing Christmas
by Allison K. García

After I came out to myself,
I had to deconstruct and
reconstruct every piece of my life

Who am I?
Who is God?
What is love?
What is family?

One moment to the next, I am
Constantly re-evaluating
Recalculating
Reconfiguring

Now we are a broken family
And a blended one
Loving and grieving

What does that mean for my memories?
My traditions?
What do we pass on to the next generation?

How do we blend Santa and Jesus for the
children?
How do we do presents?

Why do we do them?
And with whom?

What ornaments do we keep?
The one with the bride and groom from a former
marriage?
The ones with a white baby Jesus?
What message does that send my brown son?

What was once a fun, holiday classic
Is now patriarchal
Heteronormative
Outdated

We have Santa and the Grinch and elves on
shelves
And Jesus and wise men and angels
And Elsa and Frosty and Rudolph and God-
knows-what-else
Smashed together
In one space

Do we throw it all away and
Start from scratch?
Do we leave it all and let the kids decide?
Do we pick and choose?
And what does that mean for my heart?

There are so many conversations
To be had as a family
And within myself

Conversations of things passed down
Fed and swallowed
By older generations
As their duty
Their right
Their unwavering belief

But I waver
And maybe not so much waver
But question
Examine
Observe

I don't take every pill given to me
And swallow blindly

Besides, my elders taught me
To ask questions
To be loving
But with caveats
Apparently

Stranger danger
Secret words

Don't always trust
Unless it'll make the family look bad

Everyone is equal
Love your neighbor
But don't stir the pot
Don't change the system

They wonder why we question
And believe in equality
Then they drag us through the mud every day
For what they taught us

But that's neither here nor there

Can't talk about politics or religion
That's another thing they said

But I was always a rebel
Bringing up taboo topics
At family holidays

Why stop now?

Therefore, I continue to question
The whys of our traditions,
Decide what things need to be
Tossed out forever

And what can stay

So, what do I believe?

God came down as a baby
God wanted to get us
In a human way
To walk in our shoes

Christmas was an action
It was and is about loving fully
And unconditionally

Everything else is merely ornamental

Too many ornaments will distract
From the beauty of the tree
And drag its branches down

We need to examine each ornament before
carefully placing
To hold love in the balance

In the end, no matter how much I deconstruct
The foundation of it all is love

Rebirth in Bethlehem
by Ha Na Park

Every year on Christmas Eve, we take a trip to Bethlehem in our imaginations as we hear the nativity stories once again. We journey back to the Bethlehem of over 2000 years ago, through a Christmas pageant, Bible readings, the carols sung - reliving a past which still lives in the present tense, inspiring in people's hearts a sense of hope and joy that a new birth is always possible.

Tonight's story also takes us on a reflective pilgrimage to Bethlehem, following the steps of the exhausted travelers, Joseph and a very pregnant Mary, heading to Bethlehem to register their family in the census. This is no vacation jaunt to the old hometown. Caesar Augustus has spoken; everybody has to register in the town of their ancestry. In Pieter Bruegel's painting The Numbering at Bethlehem, one has to search hard to find Mary and Joseph among the village folk crowding into town. They have faded into the anonymity of the powerless. They are faceless nobodies under the boot of an uncaring Empire. There's a sense of fright and oppression in the air: first, Mary and Joseph are refused shelter, then find a place in a stable, and hear their first child's cry of birth break the silent night in their tiny, animal-scented refuge.

I see this beloved Christmas story, this particular scene of the nativity story, from the perspective of people on the move, engaging in migration, relocation and dislocation. I boarded a flight to Canada from Korea in 2006, just a few days before Christmas, carrying my passport and my seven-month-old son. My partner, Min Goo, had already arrived in Vancouver to find us a home before we joined him. Our first home in Canada was a small apartment on a street near a big shopping mall; our first Christmas in Canada had the same sense of dislocation that Mary and Joseph must have felt.

When I was young, Christmas meant going to Christmas Eve service with my parents. My father taught my brother and I how to show our adoration to the baby Jesus, lifting us up to his shoulders as he approached the nativity scene set up beside a Christmas tree at the church, to look into it carefully and appreciate the small figures in it. He would say, "There's a story.", as he taught us what their hands, body language and faces could tell us about the night of Jesus' birth. The little figures of Mary, Joseph, Jesus, shepherds, lambs, cows, angels all looked very calm and still. I tried to study their faces and hands, yet, to me, they were no more than delicately made porcelain dolls or wooden miniatures. They didn't tell me a story. They didn't move. They were keeping their warm, yet still peace, like Jesus on the Cross, hung at the front of the church, or the statue of Mary which greeted me every time I entered the sanctuary. To me, that Christmas Eve scene was as if the big statues became the small figures in the nativity - they looked the same as each other, different from me- they all had the faces of 'Westerners.': pretty faces, long eyelids, high nose, pink cheeks. I contemplated the still peace they made: What stories are they telling me?

I still wonder what the Christmas story can teach us. Like Mary and Joseph moving to Bethlehem for their family's registration according to the Emperor's decree, people in our world often struggle to find their place, their purpose. They protect their family. They move. They go. They relocate themselves, or are forcibly relocated. Dislocation is very much a part of human history globally, in our world, right now. People are forced to leave their homes by war, occupation, violence, injustice inflicted on their lives. We think of Mary and Joseph as people whose lives were made perfect by the birth of Jesus, but Mary and Joseph and the infant Jesus were refugee themselves when they left the Bethlehem they had just settled into to flee to Egypt in order to protect their son from the schemes of the murderous Herod.

Taking a pilgrimage to Bethlehem through stories helps us to contemplate the deep realities of our lives and of our world – reflecting on both the light and the darkness, hope and suffering, resistance and oppression – the context of all people and the context of the birth of Jesus. We learn why we need to hope, learn that 'hoping' and 'anticipating' for a new birth can live in the present tense, right here, right now.

When I was young, Bethlehem was simply a small town where Jesus was born in a fairy-tale-like story, coloured by the angel's and the shepherds' joy, resounding with thundering praise from the heaven by a multitude of heavenly host, with a mysterious and solitary star that guides the three Kings. Bethlehem was the place where all the mysteries happened, leading to the birth of the holy child that takes us on a journey that will change us from the inside out.

We all journey to a Bethlehem of our own. A pilgrimage of heart and mind is involved as we hold this night in silence and adoration. Bethlehem is multi-dimensional; the Bethlehem of over 2000 years ago and of 2014 co-exist as we open our eyes and hearts to the struggle of the Palestinians, cast into darkness by the separation walls that cast long shadows upon their lands. Bethlehem is the symbol of any place which is in need of *rebirth*, an impregnation of hope and vital peace. The Christmas story carries sorrow as well as joy, telling us of the darkness in humanity as well as the divinity that is born among us as an infant, the purest and most innocent form of humanity.

Tonight, may our Christmas story open our hearts to a journey of rebirth in Bethlehem; may it inspire us to throw open the gates of that little town for all to enter in.

Tradition.
by Joya Polk

I can't say that there is much to be had.
Maybe it would be that we pull out the fine china
and crystal glasses every year
And drink coke out of them.
Maybe it would be the cake and singing happy
birthday to Jesus
And the Christmas Story after.
Maybe my parents attempts at tradition were
whack.
Maybe that's all it was.
Maybe I never enjoyed any of it at all.
Maybe I did and I've erased that,
Swiped it away like clearing a thanksgiving table.
Maybe I removed those memories like lights on a
tree in January.
Maybe maybe maybe.

But perhaps I've outgrown those childish
formalities.
Childish because they were acceptable when I was
young,
When I didn't know any better.
Formalities because I felt like I had to do them to
survive,
To make it out.

But we grow.
And we learn.
And we suffer no more at the hand of
"Tradition."

I've gained a new understanding now that I'm not
small.
Now that I'm not trapped.
Now that I have a person and a house of my own.
Maybe
Maybe I don't want to keep my family's traditions.
Maybe I've learned that the burden of memory is
not worth its weight in gold.
Or frankincense.
Or myrrh.
That they're not cute trinkets to keep in a box and
display in a window every year.
Trauma is not a gift.

I have new rituals now.
And they may not be the same every year.
But they are not shameful.
They are not traumatizing.
They are free.

I am celebratory.
And I am free.

Reflection: The Lungs of Prophecy
by Ha Na Park

In the past, I often felt that the reading from Luke 3: 1-6, one of the staples of the Advent lectionary, is a disturbing text. Disturbing – and problematic for us, who live in the 21st century. We've witnessed the catastrophic consequences of giving ourselves unlimited power to alter nature according to human needs and greed. Make nature's path "straight... Every valley shall be filled... Every mountain and hill shall be made low... The crooked shall be made straight... And the rough ways made smooth." Whenever I read this passage, I could not think of anything but images of big construction projects. Dividing the mountains and cutting the hills to build a highway. Splitting natural habitats and living water's course; shutting down nature for man's convenience. I often thought, "This can't be the only picture for us to envision how to prepare the way of God!" I have long admired the protesters who fight to preserve and protect nature from the unfettered human desire to accumulate wealth. In Korea. In Canada. In and around the world. I especially admire the fight for Indigenous rights to the land, culture and self-governance. This passage hits me in the wrong way; I've even tried to skip today's Advent lectionary in the past. Some phrases make sense to us, Winter-peggers. Pot holes should be filled. I do enjoy the thrill (?) and fun of driving in Winnipeg. Sometimes it feels like I am driving a horse-drawn wagon or riding an old train. Clattering. Rattling. We do have rough roads that could be made smooth. Not to mention we already have no mountains or hills to make low. But, I wonder what could be an alternative image for God's way, truly as "the voice of one crying out in the wilderness", that would not require a bulldozer to prepare a path for God.

Originally, the mountains and hills to be made low in Isaiah are analogous to the kings. The power and principalities who rule over the valleys - - the disenfranchised, those who suffer from oppression and despair. In today's reading, these mountains are presented with many names: Tiberius, Pilate, Herod, Philip, Lysania, Annas, Caiaphas. John the Baptist sends a clear message for us: The earthly powers are corrupt, and God will intervene to "Bring down the powerful from their thrones." (1:52) In this sense, with Isaiah, John the Baptist visualizes God's ground-breaking redesign of the landscape, so much more than just repairing potholes and well-worn ruts. The voice of one crying out in the wilderness is to prepare us for the arrival of a transforming God, by constructing a highway of peace, a Skytrain of the new spirit.

As we journey this Advent, with the theme of seeking the spirit, this week, the spirit of peace, holding everyone and every creature on earth, I call us to reimagine the land work, how to prepare God's path, whose process itself is peace-building and healing.

This year, I have been reading "The Body Keeps the Score: Brain, Mind, and Body in the Healing of Trauma" by Bessel Van Der Kolk, at my friend's high recommendation. It beautifully demonstrates to me how the path to peace can be possible for trauma survivors, freeing them from the tyranny of the past through healing with "body", not just talk therapy. There are many forms such as neurofeedback, theater, meditation, play, and yoga.

Have you tried stretching your body lately? How many of you have been enjoying yoga or other physical exercise? Many traditional physical and spiritual practices teach us how to breathe in and out while moving our bodies to achieve the maximum benefit, for health and healing of our mind and spirit, along with our bodies being stretched, supported, strengthened.

When I was reading chapter 16: Learning to Inhabit your Body: Yoga, I knew I would want to share it with Immanuel, especially in the Advent season. I highlighted some insights and research in my journal, and saved them for sharing when I would have the opportunity to talk about peace. I hope that this is a helpful reminder for us as we, together and individually, seek the spirit of peace.

Here are some quotes:

> "When people are chronically angry or scared, constant muscle tension ultimately leads to spasms, back pain, migraine headaches, fibromyalgia, and other forms of chronic pain."

> "Our involvement with yoga started in 1998 when we first heard about a new biological marker, heart rate variability (HRV), that had recently been discovered to be a good measure of how well the autonomic nervous system is working. ... The autonomic nervous system is our brain's most elementary survival system, its two branches regulating arousal throughout the body. Roughly speaking, the sympathetic nervous system (SNS) uses chemicals like adrenaline to fuel the body and brain to take action, while the parasympathetic nervous system (PNS) uses acetylcholine to help regulate basic

body functions like digestion, wound healing, and sleep and dream cycles.

When we're at our best, these two systems work closely together to keep us in an optimal state of engagement with our environment and with ourselves. Heart rate variability measures the relative balance between the sympathetic and the parasympathetic systems.

When we inhale, we stimulate the sympathetic nervous system (SNS), which results in an increase in heart rate. Exhalations stimulate the parasympathetic nervous system (PNS), which decreases how fast the heart beats. In healthy individuals, inhalations and exhalations produce steady, rhythmical fluctuations in heart rate: Good heart rate variability is a measure of basic well-being." [2]

I was deeply interested in the idea that this awareness of our body as a way of trauma healing highlighted the importance of breathing, and showed us how exhalations, the moments when we breathe out, are connected to the Parasympathetic

---

[2] *The Body Keeps the Score: Brain, Mind, and Body in the Healing of Trauma* by Bessel Van Der Kolk

nervous system (PNS) that is engaged in wound healing, sleep and dreams! I thought that was very cool! 'I would pay more attention whenever I can be mindful of breathing out! I am doing something that promotes wound healing and dreams, just by breathing!!!' I immediately thought of Joseph's dream in the Nativity story. What if we see Joseph's dream in which the Angel visits him and tells him to accept Mary, not just as God's instruction, but as a wound healing, God freeing Joseph from fear through this body work called dreaming. Joseph's dream becomes exhalating; exhalating his fear which meets with God who inspires.

Prophecy as respiration, regulating and steadying our heart rates, tuned to God's rhythm! Balance, peace, wound healing, dreaming!

This new insight helped me to envision today's prophecy — "Prepare the way of God, making the path straight." — in the image of our lungs. "Making God's way straight" — I memorized the verse, like a mantra, when I started my stretching routine at night or early in the morning. It is very important, when you stretch your body, to use breathing as a way to guide it.

lung.ca explains how our lungs work. Imagine with me with these pictures - how lungs and other organs work when we breathe in and out: our mouth, nose, windpipe, the muscles in our chest — our lungs' contraction and expansion, flattening and relaxing, analogous to filling the valleys and lowering the mountains in order to prepare the path of peace.

To get the oxygen our body needs, we inhale air through our mouth and nose. The mucous membranes in our mouth and nose warm and moisten the air, and trap particles of foreign matter like dirt and dust. The air passes through the throat into the trachea (windpipe). The trachea divides into the left and right bronchi. Like a branch, each bronchus divides again and again, becoming narrower and narrower. (Note: the theme of this second Advent Sunday is "the branch of peace!" after "the bud of hope")

Our smallest airways end in the alveoli, small, thin air sacs that are arranged in clusters like bunches of balloons. When we breathe in by enlarging the chest cage, the "balloons" expand as air rushes in to fill the vacuum. When you breathe out, the "balloons" relax and air moves out of the lungs. Imagine with me, air as God's breath, peace; the membranes in our mouth and nose as the scripture; the windpipe as worship; "like a branch" each bronchus (God's Word) divides again and again, becoming narrower and narrower. The air sacs, the balloons, as the communities of faith. The communities of God's Love.

Now, tiny blood vessels surround each of the 300 million alveoli in the lungs. Oxygen moves across the walls of the air sacs, is picked up by the blood and carried to the rest of the body. It is God's love, peace, joy and hope being carried by the faithful people of God to the world. To breathe in God's spirit, we must let God inspire us – the root of 'inspiration' means to 'breathe into'. There is no breath of faith without inspiration. As we stretch ourselves during Advent, we make a straight path for the breath of God, into our lungs, into our hearts and thinking and prayer.

"Prepare the way of the Lord,

 make God's paths straight.

Every valley shall be filled,

  and every mountain and hill

shall be made low."

Home Hunting
by Meagan Ruby Wagner

Right around the corner there
I can almost see it
Your new place
An old oak on the front lawn
A dusting of snow
Porch swing in need of paint
And your boyfriend
Waiting by the door
Drink in hand
To welcome you home
From work
On a mundane Tuesday night
The week before Christmas
And I know right now
Life is dark and ugly
You don't fit with the other boys
And you feel like you will never be found
But I am here to tell you
That is not true
You are already found
And known
And loved
And someday soon
You will settle into your life
And it will be so beautiful

You almost won't believe it
So wait it out with me
I will hold a candle in the dark and
Wait with you
While you figure out
How to make your life
A home

Candles in the Windows
by Henry J. Barnosky

A long time ago, when I was just starting to realize that I was some sort of man, I'd go out walking in the dead of night.

Every year, without fail, I think of those cold winter evenings. God had been working in my life so well and so thoroughly that I'd forgotten how to be afraid of death. I'd walk downtown without a thought for my own safety, to go out into the wide English countryside where the farmland spread out in every direction. Sometimes I'd sing at the top of my lungs, and sometimes I'd walk in silence. Mostly, though, I'd pray, and when I came home up the long, winding road to the Lodge, I would see light from the windows spilling out across the snow, and I'd know that I was loved.

Candles in the windows. It was never important to me to have candles in the windows at Christmastime until I returned to New England, with the memory of that Christmas spent abroad studying Christ's words still glowing in my heart. It was a Christmas spent in the warm embrace of close friends. Hot chocolate and caroling, flickering fireplaces, the smell of mincemeat pies waking me up on a lazy Sunday morning while the snow fell. It was an idyllic, Heaven-sent Christmas. A picture postcard Christmas.

It was also the last Christmas I'd celebrate with the name I'd been born under, and the last Christmas I'd spend loved and held close by any sort of Christian community.

The difference was painful and brutally stark. Christmas became a cold and lonely thing, something I couldn't celebrate with the Church- not with my patchy facial hair and deepening voice- and something I couldn't celebrate with any of my newfound queer acquaintances, who hated Christians and everything to do with them. Silent nights, holy nights. Me and my tree and my prayers, and my door that stayed locked after nightfall. No more walking.

I dreamed of going back to England. To me this symbolized, in some way, going back to missions. But my chances of getting back in with that organization were slim to none. I could only hope and pray that God did not dwell only on English roads at midnight; that He'd followed me home, and would continue to follow me, no matter where I went or how I wandered.

God and my own queer identity were indelibly intertwined. If He hadn't all but spoken to me so many years ago, and told me that *yes, yes, I made you as you are, and I love you for it-* if He hadn't done that, I would not have become the man I am today. What was the first moment, I wonder, when I first knew that to be a man who loved men was holy? When I learned, through gender transition and finally stepping into my manhood, that the human body is a temple unto God? When I looked once more at a Christian place of worship, and finally saw the candles in the windows?

It could have been the first time I saw a queer, Christian man portrayed on screen. It could have been the first time I looked at the story of the Centurion with new eyes, or the first queer poet I read who spoke about God not with fear or hatred, but with love and reverence.

But personally, I think it was Christmas day. When my mother, who loved God relentlessly and loved me just the same, hung a new ornament on the tree. My name. *My name.* My name hung proudly in a place of honor on the tree in the corner of the living room.

I touched it. Held the ornament in my hands. It was very light, but it felt very, very heavy. Weighted with promise, with the meaning it held, with the ideas it sparked. And just like that, I saw a lifetime of Christmases laid out before me. A lifetime of candles in windows, and Christmas lights, and a queer, Christian man who might kiss me and whisper, "Merry Christmas. God be with you."

For once, that marriage between the queer and the sacred did not seem so impossible. At last, it seemed not only possible, but divinely ordained. All that from an ornament, made by someone who loved me, and hung on a Christmas tree for everyone to see.

In God's house, there is a place on the tree for me, and for you. Even if there isn't a place in the Church, or in the parade. In God's house, the snow falls just right, and we can go out walking at any hour without fear.

In God's house, there are always candles in the windows.

Christmas Angel
by Ziel

It is Christmas, and I am an angel
And I am to be on a thousand trees
Feeling a thousand shocks of joy
Instead I am here
In the cold
And I have only two eyes
And no wings
Still no wings

A Simple Family Christmas
by Raelee May Carpenter

[Content Warning: homophobic and transphobic speech]

Dani had never seen Mayra's eyes so wide, and he couldn't help grinning. The diner was strung with so many rainbow-colored Christmas lights it looked like a gingerbread house. Daniel and Riv's daughter was so excited about it she'd barely noticed her pureed bananas, which she usually loved.

"Mayra Grace," he said, "bite."

The baby opened her mouth wide enough for Dani to tilt in some of her dessert, but most of it still slid down her chin. Daniel caught what he could and redirected it into her mouth. He shot his spouse a look and shrugged.

"*Esta bien*[3]." Riv tossed back the last bite of their BBQ burger and twirled the lid back onto Mayra's

---

[3] It's okay.

half-full jar of chicken and gravy. *"Hay cereal si decide que tiene hambre[4]."*

Yeah. There was cereal scattered all over the table, because Lil MG hardly had touched her Cheerios either. Distraction: 3, lunch: 0. But Daniel handed River the jar of bananas and the sticky spoon, and they grabbed a plastic zipper bag from Mayra's pink tote.

"Sit, honey." Riv tucked the baggie into the tote and patted Dani's shoulder.

"I am."

"I mean really."

Dani settled back into his chair to attack his vegetarian omelet. Daniel had been so distracted with his daughter's lunch he'd only eaten half of his own. River sat back down and smiled at Dani.

"May I get you all anything else?" The server was a young native girl, and super-attentive. She'd earned the generous tip Daniel was adding in his head.

---

[4] There's cereal if she decides she's hungry.

River dredged their last onion ring through a puddle of ketchup, but didn't break gaze with Dani. "I'm dying for that brownie sundae. What do you think?"

Daniel had never understood his spouse's appetite. "You go ahead. I'm good."

"We can split it."

"Maybe I'll eat a couple bites."

The waitress grinned. "Two spoons. Holiday sprinkles?"

Daniel's eyebrows went up involuntarily.

"Of course!" said River.

She winked at Dani. "Be right back."

Under the table, a calloused hand caressed Dani's thigh. Daniel smiled back at River, but even after all these years together, he couldn't hide his blush at Riv's public affection...or his private response to it. He squeezed Riv's knee, then lifted another bite of egg and veggies to his mouth.

"What a cute little elf you have here! I could just eat him up."

If Riv noticed the stranger had mis-gendered their baby, they didn't say so. In River's mind, Mayra was far too young to settle on a gender. As Daniel chewed, he looked up at the middle aged white woman, but she was lost in his spouse's blue eyes. He understood the feeling, but...

River gazed at Mayra, those eyes glowing. "Thank you. I wanted to make elf ears too, but Daniel said she'd only take them off and try to eat them." Of course Lil MG's holiday santa-photo-and-shopping outfit had been of Riv's styling. Long-sleeve Kelly-green onesie with fuzzy scarlet leggings. Her matching striped cap, a gift from Dani's oldest sister Valeria, had a gold felt faux-bell sewn at the end.

River tensed noticeably—well, noticeable to Daniel anyway—when the lady grabbed the fugazi bell on their daughter's hat and waved it around. Dani pursed his lips. Before entering the distracting gingerbread diner, that bell had spent most of its day in Mayra's mouth.

"Danielle? Is that his mommy?" The woman leaned down and blew a raspberry against MG's fat cheek.

Daniel's spouse, subtly as they could, tugged the chair with Mayra's booster seat closer to their own chair. River did NOT like it when strangers touched their kid. "*I'm* Mommy," said River.

The stranger laughed. "No, honey. You're the *daddy*."

Good thing she wasn't looking at Dani, because he couldn't help the eye-roll. *Please straightsplain strict binary gender roles to my queer spouse in a public restaurant. That's exactly what we want for Christmas this year.*

"I'm that sometimes too." Mayra's chair inched even closer to River's.

Now that the felt bell had been brought back to Mayra's attention, it was in her mouth again. The hat had been tugged off without ceremony and left her black hair going in every direction. The woman tried to smooth straight the baby's impossible curls, and River cleared their throat. She looked up at them. The booster seat was practically in Riv's lap by now.

River laid a hand on Dani's shoulder. "This is Daniel, my husband."

"Oh." The strange woman looked at Daniel, as if seeing him for the first time only after having familiar contact with his child three times. Her hand drew back from Mayra like the child's head was a hot stove.

"Hello, happy holidays." Daniel's voice was as cheerful as he could manage.

She looked from Dani to River and back. "Well, I'm sorry, but this is just wrong. Babies need Mommies and Daddies. Otherwise, they really get cheated in life."

Daniel and River looked at each other. The words "B___, you don't know our life" could have been tattooed on Riv's forehead. A lot of babies didn't have Daddies. Mayra lived with two parents who were crazy about her! She also received regular contact with Valeria, who'd donated the egg, and Clarity, their gestational surrogate. Not to mention the host of aunts and uncles—biological, foster, and volunteer—who doted on her, prayed for her, and brought her gifts. But Dani bit his lip.

"And here we are!" The waitress nudged the woman aside and laid the holiday-decorated brownie sundae, fresh forks, and extra napkins out on the table with the flourish of a Vegas illusionist.

"Thank you so much." Daniel gave their server a grateful grin.

The strange Karen couldn't take a hint. "You're just going to serve them?"

The smile the server turned on the nosy patron was tight. "How can I help you?"

"These men don't have a mother for this poor little boy."

"Ma'am, I'm going to ask you to return to your table and not disturb other diners." The server turned back to Dani and Riv, partially to ask if they wanted anything else but partially—Dani was convinced—to act as a human shield between them and the annoying Karen.

The strange woman, who'd been joined by two others, tapped the server on the shoulder. "But this is a family restaurant—"

"And this is family is eating lunch just like every other family. If you can't leave them in peace to enjoy their dessert, I'm going to ask you leave the diner."

"My friends and I just ordered our food!"

"Thanks for letting us know. We'll cancel that right away."

"But—!"

The chef—a native man who could've been an NFL linebacker—leaned out of the kitchen window. "What's up, Jess?"

"Cancel the order on table...five."

"Well, I never." One of the late-comer Karens *literally* clutched her pearls. Though the pearls themselves were about as real as the "gold" bell on his daughter's hat.

"Got it." Chef ripped a green check off the order holder. "Do you need me to come out?"

Already, the three women were gathering shopping bags from under their table. As they scurried out the door, one shouted back, "We wouldn't eat here if it was the last restaurant in Laughlin! In all of Nevada!"

As the door closed behind Karen Party of Three, several diners broke into spontaneous applause. Dani smiled and looked at Riv.

River wasn't smiling. They poked at the chocolate brownie goodness with a distinctly un-Riv-like lack of enthusiasm. Mayra reached toward the dessert, and after Daniel distracted her with a rice cracker, he looked up to see the server—Jess—still standing by, frowning.

"I am so sorry, you guys," she said. "Is there anything else I can do?"

Dani ran his fingers through River's hair then nodded. "Actually, could you pack this up? It looks amazing, but we're gonna head home."

"Of course. Right away." Jess picked up the plate and headed back to the kitchen.

∞

River stared down at their hands. The scenery passing out the car window had made them dizzy. Finally, they took a breath. "I'm sorry. I ruined it."

"No, honey." Daniel sighed. "It was a good day. A lot of good memories. That last thing…"

Riv's husband only shrugged. What was there to say? That stuff happened all the time. River should be used to it by now, but it still hurt.

Even though Jess, the waitress, had stood up for them. Even though she'd brought brand new warm brownies and ice cream packed in separate insulated containers. Even though she'd told them another patron had paid their bill, and that she would have if someone else hadn't.

It still hurt.

River would have paid the bill ten times over just to eat a burger and brownie in peace with their husband and daughter. To have people treat their little family just like the others. A cute baby for smiling but not for touching uninvited. A loving married couple to be congratulated and wished a happy Christmas, not told they were cheating their daughter.

"What if she's right?" Riv couldn't even hold the words back. "What if our baby is missing out, not having a real mom? A real family. Missing that love…"

Dani reached over to tweak River's ear tenderly. "Are you kidding? Valeria, Clarity, our folks, all the Diaz kids? My sisters, Sean, Glo, Djalu, Ana, Mr. and Mrs. Sanchez? I could go on for days, Papi. Our family is real as any, and Mayra has more love than any baby I've ever known."

Riv laughed, but only slightly. "You're right."

"I know it's hard, dealing with crap like that. But Lil MG…she's happy. Please, mi amor, don't worry about our kid."

"I'll try." But as excited as River had been for the holiday family outing, they were relieved when Dani pulled the Mustang into the driveway of their cozy adobe house on the outskirts of Needles, California. The town was small, but it had been mostly welcoming since River moved there as a fifteen-year-old refugee from South America. The people who hadn't been comfortable with Riv at first had gotten used to them over the last ten years.

Wow. It had really been that long. Eleven years this past fall, actually. It wasn't perfect, but it was home. Laughlin was far more touristy than Needles, and when they trekked up to the outlets…well, they never knew who they'd meet.

"We can't hide in our house all the time." Dani. With sacks of Christmas shopping tucked under one arm and the baby carrier hanging from the other.

Daniel couldn't read Riv's mind, but he'd known them from the day they arrived in Needles. He knew enough.

"I know." Riv had only thought to bring the brownies and ice cream from the car, so they stopped for the mail, just to even things out a bit. The box was stuffed. In addition to the regular bills and a couple late-ish holiday catalogues, there were several cards (Dani was right; their family was loved) and a large padded envelope.

Oh. The Christmas package from Clarity, who'd carried Mayra before birth. She'd texted Riv that this was coming.

Daniel had met Clarity in college at UNLV, but River had developed a strong connection with her on the weekend visits they made to see Dani in Vegas. Even for the months the two had broken up, she'd kept up with River. When Clarity moved back to Hawaii after graduation, staying in touch seemed natural.

Now that Mayra was here, Clarity was no longer a friend, but forever family.

River followed their husband into the house and stowed away the aborted dessert for a better moment later. While Dani went out to get the last few shopping bags, Riv got dozy Mayra out of the carrier and into her playpen.

Then they texted Clarity. *Present is here. Thank you much.*

A few seconds later their phone chimed. *Nooo!!! Did you open it?*

Riv chuckled. *We JUST walked in the door.*

Good. I'm Skyping in.

"Dani!" River called. They knew Clarity would want to be together—virtually, at least—while they opened her gift.

"Here." Right over their shoulder.

Riv jumped.

"Sorry. Didn't mean to sneak up."

They waved off his apology. River must've shouted right in his ear. "Clarity's package came."

"I see."

The call tone came. Riv tapped the button, and the lovely face of their daughter's tummy-mama appeared on the screen.

"Hey, beautifuls. Merry Christmas."

The three chatted for only a minute before Clarity chided, "Okay, open it, open it."

The guys laughed. Patience wasn't Clarity's thing, but Riv didn't need to be told twice either. They ripped at the tab and turned the envelope over. A flurry of navy and fluorescent pink slid out.

An aloha shirt! Pink pineapples on navy background. With a tiny matching dress and bucket hat for the baby! A couple sizes up from where she was now, the outfit would fit just right come summer. For Dani, a handsome, fitted navy polo with a pink pineapple embroidered on the pocket.

"What do you think?" Clarity asked.

River swallowed hard.

"I thought of you, Riv, when I saw that shirt. Then the rest just…came together."

"Wow, geez," said Dani. "It's like you know us or something."

"You think so, Daniel? You okay, Riv?"

Riv nodded and wiped at a getaway tear. "Es perfecta. All perfect."

Two Advents

by Avery Arden

As a child packs a snowball
tight and firm and
cold seeping even through their mittens
into palms

so You
once packed the Universe
into a ball scarce larger than
the pomegranates that had yet to burst
into being…

But still a greater miracle awaited!
— a denser packing of Infinity
into small single atoms —
You! You

curled Your endless Being up
into an embryo

oh! You who grew
the cosmos on a particle of Breath

You packed Yourself down into
near nothingness —
and waited.

You waited there
in warm dark roundness till
the time had come for Her to birth you,
wet and bloody, into an uncaring world.

Somehow
the Being who could wear the galaxy
like a bangle
nursed and grew and toddled,
walked among
us tiny beings of the frail bones…

i'll never, ever
ever fathom it.

Divinity! if i could hold You now
as Mary held you, in my quaking arms
i think i might just know *why* You sustain

each instant — now, and now, and now again —
all of existence.

Seed upon the palm
tucked lovingly into a rich dark soil

infant on the breast
fed lovingly from one's own aching flesh

— but not yet. Not yet —
already, yes — and still
not yet.

with Earth i wait for You
with bated breath.

About this poem:

When I wrote this piece in 2019, I had been
going through a time of spiritual stagnancy as
religious trauma caught up to me…so it was a gift
to awaken a little after midnight on the first Sunday
of Advent with images of Divinity and Roundness
glowing in my heart like embers, reminding me of
birth and rebirth and the eternal sustaining breath
of God.

The Creation and the Incarnation are
intertwined for me — when I think of God birthing
the universe, my mind eventually wanders to the
human who birthed God, and vice-versa. And
through the way our liturgical year returns us over
and over to the story of God's entering into Hir
good, good world; and the story of God's creative
act lasting not an instant but over all ages, I think of
Meister Eckhart's declaration:

> *"What does God do all day long? God gives birth. From the beginning of eternity, God lies on a maternity bed giving birth to all. God is creating this whole universe full and entire in this present moment."*

Let me leave you with some notes about various images in this poem:

On the image of the pomegranate for the Big Bang event — have you ever sliced into a pomegranate and pulled the halves apart with enough force for those rich ruby seeds within to fling themselves upward, sideways, all about? That bright explosion is to me a fitting image for that first flinging of dust into infant stars, scattered across black space.

"...the Being who could wear the galaxy / like a bangle..." — this line is inspired by Bengali poet Rabindranath Tagore's depiction of the Lord of the Dance, Shiva, with celestial bodies whirling round his dancing ankles. You can find out more about that poem, and see some gorgeous art that fuses Hindu and Christian tradition, at tinyurl.com/2mrpp455. For now, here are the most relevant lines from Tagore's poem:

> *"Rebellious atoms are subdued into forms at thy dance-time,*

the suns and planets, anklets of light, twirl
round thy moving feet, and,

age after age, things struggle to wake from
dark slumber,

through pain of life, into consciousness,

and the ocean of thy bliss breaks out in
tumults of suffering and joy."

In Hindu tradition, Shiva's dance is the source of all movement in the universe; it also frees humanity from ignorance and illusion. This conception of Divinity as Dancer resonates deeply with me, and links well in my mind to the Big Bang event — a dance begun long eons ago continues into the present and for all time, ever sustaining and constantly transforming the cosmos that Divinity so loves.

"...seed upon the palm..." — We return to the image of a seed, but this time it's the hazelnut of Julian of Norwich's visions. In her vision, Christ hands Julian a ball no larger than a hazelnut and tells her that all of Creation is contained within that small globe. Julian describes the experience thus:

"I was amazed that it could last, for I
thought that because of its littleness it
would suddenly have fallen to nothing. And

> *I was answered in my understanding: 'It lasts and always will, because God loves it; and thus everything has being through the love of God.'"*

There is not a speck of matter in this universe that is *not* loved by God, that is not nurtured and watched over by its Creator, who revels in the stars and celebrates the blood pulsing through your fingertips. It is the creative energy and life-bearing power of this Love that forms and sustains each and every one of us. And it is that Love that moved God to slip off Infinity and step into flesh. Already this impossible event has taken place — and yet…we return to it yearly. Await it yearly. Yearn for it yearly. The already and not yet of God's Kin(g)dom is a Mystery that I almost begin to grasp when I think on the wonder and waiting to which we return as one, every Advent.[5]

---

[5] *This poem and essay were first shared at https://binarybreakingliturgy.com/2020/11/29/poem-for-the-first-sunday-of-advent/.*

On the Incarnation
by Blake Ellis Edwards

Often at this time of year, we jump the gun and start talking about the meaning of Christ's death and resurrection. And fair enough, that's the standard Lutheran sermon template: you need law and gospel, and the gospel is the empty tomb, after all.

But long before Luther, Christians celebrated the nativity as one of the holiest events of the year, and one of the holiest events in history. And while some of the carols make mention of the cross, most don't. Most are very fixated on the baby in the manger, and the shepherds and angels that attended his infancy. Matthew and Luke seem perfectly happy to focus on the child and not foreshadow his death too heavily.

We don't go amiss if, like our ancestors, we carve out this season of the year to focus very particularly on the child in the manger. There is gospel to be found simply in God's choice to be made flesh and dwell among us. In becoming human and inhabiting a human body, God demonstrates that our humanness, our bodily pains and pleasures, are not unclean to God. God blesses our embodied human existence by choosing to take part in it.

Maybe that's why Christmas is such an embodied holiday, full of scents and flavors and visually-pleasing décor. The sensory pleasures of Christmas can serve as a reminder each year that God is with us in our bodies, whatever they are going through inside or out.

lying in a manger
by SJ Blasko

i wonder if baby Jesus panicked
the way i do
at the cold air on his skin
the limits of how far his limbs could stretch
i wonder if he napped in boats
exhausted from the weight
of holding this borrowed frame upright
he slept through a storm
and i don't know why, exactly, but
i know i can relate
as i lay on this floor
swaddled in this blanket
so the air does not touch me
i wonder if he had comfort things
to wrap around himself and feel
(just feel)

i wonder if the way that he was human
is the way that i feel broken
(i wonder just how deep mortality cut)

Obscurity and Its Consequences
by Neil Ellis Orts

This is all pure speculation.

Every once in a while, one of my atheist or spiritual-but-not-religious friends will post an article quoting one scholar or another about how Jesus was unlikely to have been a historical figure. I seldom get involved in the subsequent thread, but will often follow it for a bit, just to see where it goes.

Now, I feel like I need to say upfront that I'm not one of those Christians that feels like he has to defend every little question about my religion. If it were possible to provide incontrovertible evidence that Mary, Joseph, Jesus and the 12 disciples were all pure works of fiction, I don't know what difference that would make to me at this point. I recognize that the age in which the Gospels were written was an age where stories were more likely to be mythologized than reported in our modern sense of the word. I've read my share of "historical Jesus" material and find it all interesting but not faith-threatening. I think if I were to have denounced Christianity, I would have done it by now. These stories, for better and worse, have shaped me, shaped my life. I made an effort some

20 years ago to dump it all and I failed. I figure I'm here to stay.

But I'm as prone to speculation as anyone and often these proclamations of the fictional nature of the Gospels rests, more or less, on one major premise: Jesus is not mentioned in any non-Biblical material, anywhere. (Well, there's the one mention of him in Josephus, but I've seen the argument that some zealous Christian added that to Josephus' history. I don't know. I wasn't there and I haven't researched that claim.)

Reading the Bible stories about Jesus, it's easy to get the impression that he was like a rock star, getting huge crowds everywhere he went, known by everyone. Did he really attract 5,000 people that one time? Having grown up near a town of just under 3,000 population, I have to say I suspect some hyperbole on the part of the gospel writers. Did Jesus' triumphant entry into Jerusalem really create traffic jams and crowded sidewalks? I suspect that, too, has some hyperbole. It was clearly enough to get the attention of the authorities, but how many would that take? I see protests here in Houston that attract law officers and there's maybe 100, 150 on those street corners. Houston has, I'm pretty sure, a much larger population than Jerusalem did at the time. If Jesus did gather a couple of hundred folk, that would have been upsetting to the power structure.

Jesus wasn't the only wandering preacher of the time. He wasn't the only figure to gain a following. One thing that Rome did well was that it squashed anything that looked the least bit threatening to their authority.

So Jesus was just another bug to step on, really. He, and John before him, may have run afoul of the powers that were, but it's hard to know how many like him there were. Jesus and the two thieves were not the only ones to be crucified, not by a long shot.

Thus my speculation goes like this: Only the few around him would have considered writing down stories about him. It was the growing numbers of people who shared the Jesus stories that made them famous. Otherwise, he was more or less just another obscure preacher with a penchant for pissing off powerful people.

In some ways, this obscurity, this hard-to-pin-down-historically aspect of Jesus fits the general point of the Incarnation. God became human, but not a famous human. Our story goes that God became this unremarkable, popular-with-the-wrong-people sort of human. Why would Jesus appear in other writings?

(Take a moment to compare the stories, rumors, and controversies about someone like William Shakespeare, who lived a more popular and public life and died only 400 years ago. History hides a lot, which leaves us to question a lot. Questions are not a bad thing, though jumping to conclusions may be.)

So, my counter-argument to "There's no evidence Jesus ever existed" is "There's very little evidence he didn't exist." Neither argument, it seems to me, is strong enough to debunk or shore up a religious faith.

What the Christian faith has is stories and a theology built up around stories. Part of the theology that emerged is our theology of incarnation. God put on flesh and/or God honored flesh in the person of Jesus. We can draw from the stories of Jesus that not only the flesh of rock stars matter, but also the flesh of someone who is not remembered except in stories his friends told. Peasant flesh. Crucified flesh. Disposable-by-empire flesh. Obscure flesh.

We speak of the humility of Christ. I firmly believe this is what it looks like.

Traditions
by Ruckus Aquinas

Self-published annual reports flooding our
mailbox
Fruitcake that comes in a box rather than out of a
closet
The sudden and exuberant veneration of all things
campy without the pretext of a drag show
Movies whose lines would win us any lip sync
challenge in which they were featured

Careful calculations about which gatherings to
attend
Where to sit at the table
How long to stay in attendance
How many escape plans to prepare beforehand
And whether to participate in competitive games
whose gilded veneer of lightheartedness
Glosses over decades-long rivalries

Jokes with your friends that subvert the innocence
of childhood holiday favorites
Providing much-needed relief between family
jokes that would collapse under their own weight
without the foundation of gender roles defined by
relatives before us

Those older relatives shoehorning you back into
those gender roles even in your rebellion against
them
Commenting about how you danced in the
Nutcracker in such a masculine way
Or how you brought a feminine touch to putting
up the holiday lights

Your deadname resurfacing
On a childhood ornament
Or a Christmas stocking
Or someone's mouth

The masks we are forced to wear of who we once
were
Lest we go unrecognized as who we presently are
by those that raised us

These holiday traditions are quite like the family
with whom we celebrate them

In that we neither chose nor look forward to them
all

Our Lady of Disgrace[6]
by Avery Arden

*[Content warning for this story: homophobia and
transphobia; (mostly unintentional) deadnaming and
misgendering; coming out to parents with less-than-
positive reactions. However, the story also includes
loving queer relationships, affirmation from faith
figures, and hope for future acceptance!]*

"You sure you're not forgetting anything on that
list of yours? Medical records? Birth certificate?"

"Check and check."

"Baby photos? Rosaries? Old diaries I can read
to unlock more of your angsty teen backstory?"

That got a laugh out of them, despite
everything. "*Yes*, babe, it's all there. But if you
secretly read those diaries, I'll replace all your
sapphic romance novels with hetero trash. ...We'll
read them together. Late at night. While stoned out
of our minds."

---

[6] For an audio version of this story read by the author, visit
https://youtu.be/pzkmkG5UYMw

"Perfect." Ellie leaned across the console to kiss her partner before they opened the passenger side door. "You *positive* you don't want me to come with you? Or at least drop you off closer?"

Joe nodded. "They think Hannah's dropping me off, so they can't see your car. Plus, this is something I have to do alone." *Well, not* alone *alone,* they thought, reflexively reaching down to pat their jacket pocket.

"Okay. I'll be right here. Just a phone call or mad dash away."

"I know. Thanks, El." Joe climbed out and made their way to the trunk. From the messy mountain of worn duffels and bulging trash-bags, they grabbed the one niceish bag — a wheeled suitcase. Lifting it from the pile was no trouble, light as it was.

As they started to head off, the whirring of a car window sliding down caused them to glance back. Their girlfriend leaned out the driver's side window, dark curls set alight by the setting sun behind her. Her smile didn't quite smooth out the worry wrinkling her brow as she called, "Your getaway car awaits, my love!"

Throat suddenly too dry to answer, Joe lifted one arm in half-acknowledgement, half-wave, and continued down the sidewalk, suitcase rolling behind them.

"I could come in with you."

"You and your brother have already done enough, Zipporah! More than enough."

Zipporah grinned that crooked grin of hers. "You sure do owe us big time." Her tone shifted from joking to earnest. "Still. I would not abandon you for this part, if you need me."

"I'm good, Zipp. I'm calm. Remember what the angel told me? With God…"

"All things are possible. Mhmm. Well, it certainly would require a miracle for a girl's parents to take her premarital pregnancy well."

"However they take it, all will turn out for good."

The two girls embraced. When they pulled apart, Zipporah held on to the other girl's arms, gazing into her eyes. "See you soon. If it doesn't go as you hope, head over tonight; I'll have fig cakes waiting."

"You're the best, Zipp."

"I know," Zipporah replied with a wink, and turned to go. "Don't forget, Aram heads out right at dawn — be ready!"

"I will be."

"And you're sure that cousin of yours won't mind you showing up unannounced?"

Elisabet's face, the laugh lines crinkling around her eyes, arose in Maryam's mind. She could almost feel the tight hug she knew her cousin would wrap her in the second she arrived, surprise or not. "Oh yes," she said. "She's always overjoyed to see me."

Despite the ache in their gut that had been growing for the last hour of their drive, Joe couldn't help a small grin as they passed the Longs' house: their grass was still the patchiest in all the neighborhood, just like Joe remembered. A couple toy guns lay abandoned among the brown leaves dotting the yard, missed by whatever perfunctory raking had taken place back in November. The tricycle Joe's memory conjured up, faded green with rusty handlebars and one pedal missing, had been replaced by an adult-size bike — also faded green, but less rusty and with no missing parts — leaning haphazardly against the closed garage door.

Wonder what they'll think, Joe mused. *Would Ms. Long have let me babysit her kids all those summer days if she'd known?* No, don't think about that! Joe shook their head vigorously, feeling their short brown hair shake around their ears. The hand not pulling the suitcase returned to their jacket pocket. Fidgeted with the zipper.

A sudden, frankly overdramatic gasp up ahead interrupted Joe's tangled thoughts. It was followed by an exclaimed name that might as well have been a sniper's bullet.

"Jennifer? Jen, is that really you?" *Ugh.* Jerking their gaze away from the Long kids' (or teens' now, Joe supposed) bike, Joe looked for the source of the voice calling out to them — though not to *them,* really.

Ah, Mrs. Rudyard. Just as they'd feared.

The middle-aged woman stood at the top of the steps to her front door, much of which was obscured by the gargantuan wreath the Rudyards hung there every year. One perfectly manicured hand shielded her eyes from the sun setting behind Joe's head; the other clutched a Michael Kors purse to her middle. Upon catching Joe's eyes, her lips parted in a wide smile showcasing perfectly white teeth. She hurried down the steps, down past the blowup Nativity taking up a big chunk of yard, and towards the curb as fast as her worryingly high heels would allow.

Joe would have loved to turn tail and run, but this lady was now right smack in between them and their destination. *No way but through*, they thought, squaring their shoulders.

"Hey, Mrs. Rudyard," they said resignedly as they slowed to a halt. "How's it going?"

"Come here, girly, let me look at you!" Mrs. Rudyard spread her arms wide as if to receive Joe in a hug, though Joe remained where they were. She looked Joe up and down so intensely that Joe glanced down at their own body, just to make sure — yep, still wearing the jacket, the skinny jeans with the scuffed hems, the grubby converse; they weren't *really* stripped naked under that appraising stare. "Ooh honey, your hair, it's…so very short!"

Joe had no clue how to respond to that statement. *Gee, how astute of you?* But just as they remembered, Mrs. Rudyard didn't need a particularly engaged conversation partner to keep talking.

"I guess short hair on girls is somewhat 'in' these days, especially among the...what do you call yourselves? Hipsters?" She tittered out that high-pitched little laugh of hers, as if she'd said something witty. Her eyes alighted on Joe's suitcase. "I suppose you just got back in town for Christmas, welcome home sweetheart!" she continued, hardly pausing for breath, let alone an answer.

"Thanks," Joe said tiredly; then, scrambling to get the words out before the woman could continue, "Well, my parents are expecting me, so..."

"Yes, yes of course! I was just on my way to Bible study anyway — at the *Baptist* church of course. I know your family is *Catholic*, which is...nice." It was incredible, really, how much condescension she could pack into a sentence.

It took all Joe's self-control not to roll their eyes as they got walking again. They settled for a "Happy *holidays,* Mrs. Rudyard," thrown over their shoulder as they left the woman and her ludicrous Nativity scene behind.

"Uh-huh, uh well yes, thank you," they heard the woman flounder behind them. "Tell your folks I say hi!"

The rest of the yards rolled by without incident. Bradleys. Shahs — no wait, they'd moved out a year or two ago; Joe had no clue who lived there now. Hensons. Detwilers. As their own house neared, Joe could swear the rumbling of the suitcase wheels got louder and louder, till it reached a fever pitch filling their mind. Their palms suddenly clammy despite the mid-December chill, the suitcase handle almost slipped from their fingers. They rearranged their grip, squeezed the handle tighter. Fine, they were fine, it was going to be fine. Or at least, it would be over soon anyway.

Their free hand moved to their pocket once again, and this time, they unzipped it. Reached in. Wrapped their fingers around the carved wood, and felt a little calmer.

They rolled their suitcase up their own driveway, approached their own front door, with its *normal* sized wreath (take note, Rudyards!) and yellow light spilling out from behind it.

Their fingers still curled around the figure in their pocket, they continued forward. Reached the front porch stairs. Paused to collapse the handle back down into the suitcase. Lifted the weightless case up the two porch steps. Reached for the doorknob.

Paused again. *My hair!* Remembering Mrs. Rudyard's comment, Joe yanked their hood up over their head. Then they reached for the doorknob once more.

It didn't turn to let them in. Locked.

As she stepped inside, she pulled off her hood, letting her dark ringlets spill out with a sigh. "Mother, father, I'm home!" she called.

"Dearest of daughters! Pupil of my eye!" She smiled at her father's voice, and her smile grew as his beard, long gone white but still thick and full, tickled her cheek when he kissed it. "How was synagogue? How are Aaron's children doing?"

Taking a deep breath, Joe knocked.

Not ten seconds passed before a silhouette blocked some of the light spilling from behind the wreath, before the click of the lock, before the door was pulled open and Joe's mom was flinging her arms around them.

"Jenny, baby, welcome home!"

"Hey, Mom," Joe mumbled into the soft gray of their mom's cashmere shoulder.

"Come in, come in, it's freezing out here!" Mom pulled Joe through the doorway. Then she yelled over her shoulder, "Simon! Jenny's home!"

Joe toed off their converse and used a foot to push them towards the shoe rack as their dad's footsteps tromped down the stairs.

"Sweetheart!" he exclaimed, and pulled Joe into a hug even tighter than their mom's had been.

"Hi, Daddy."

"Sorry I had the door locked, honey," their mom was saying as she closed the front door. "I didn't hear Hannah's car."

"Oh yeah. Um, I got dropped off at the end of the street. Wanted to stretch my legs." It wasn't a lie. Just a half-truth.

"How is Hannah? How was the trip?" Dad asked as he released Joe from the crushing hug.

"Oh, we heard the news!" their mom interrupted before Joe could come up with something. "It's *so* exciting, and weren't those engagement photos just beautiful? What's her *beau's* name again?"

"Um..." Joe racked their brain for that Facebook post they'd scrolled past last month.

"Dave, wasn't it?" their dad answered, thankfully. "Nice boy from up in Tennessee?"

"That's right, Dave!" Mom exclaimed, clapping her hands together. "I'm so darn happy for them both. Speaking of..." she focused on Joe again. "You don't have a happy surprise for us, I suppose? A boyfriend of your own...?"

"God, no!" Joe hadn't meant it to come out so curt and, well, definitive, but there it was.

"Jennifer," Mom warned, and Joe tried not to wince at both the name and the tone. *Thou shalt not take the Lord's name in vain under* my *roof,* right, right.

"Hey, why are we standing here barely inside the house?" Dad cut in quickly. "Jenny, let's get you to the kitchen and get some good home cooking in you."

"Oh yes, Daddy made your favorite!" their mom chimed in, relieved to leave the tense moment behind. "It's in the warming drawer waiting for you."

"Thanks Daddy, that's real nice of you," Joe said, and tried to mean it. "I'm just gonna take my bag upstairs first, use the bathroom."

"I'll get your bag," Dad offered, reaching for the suitcase.

"No!" Again, they didn't mean to be so curt. "Uh, that's okay, Daddy. I got it." They lifted the suitcase, trying to make out like it was heavier than it was, and started to carry it up the stairs. "See y'all in a minute."

"I expect that hood down at the table, sweetie!" their mom called after them.

The door to Joe's bedroom was open, the ceiling light on. They tried not to bristle at that; Mom had probably just gone in to freshen up the sheets or whatever. Still, first thing they did after plopping the suitcase down on the bed was to pull open the dresser's bottom drawer, dig around in the jumble of old clothes — mostly t-shirts from grade school theatre and writing clubs — and pull out the shoebox buried beneath.

Without opening the lid, they lifted the box up to eye level and tilted till they spied…*yes*, there it was: the strand of hair was still in place, undisturbed. Breathing a sigh of relief, they deposited the shoe box beside their suitcase and opened it. The strand of hair tumbled from where they had carefully tucked it a few years back, just under the lid. Joe wouldn't need that security measure to alert them to any parental snooping anymore.

They pulled out one of the notebooks inside, smiling softly at the big bold TOP SECRET! KEEP OUT! message their pre-teen self had scrawled with a jumbo sharpie. Joe rifled through the pages, stopped at a random point, and scanned the page idly.

"Dear Diary. I want to f#^%!ng die." Yep, they'd actually censored the word like it was in a comic strip — as if that would have kept Mom from grounding them for using it if she'd seen. "My boobs are coming in faster and faster and Mom says I need to start wearing a bra. YACK!!! WHY can't my body just stay the same forever? Puberty is such

B.S. ...Also. If a boy snaps my bra strap I'll SNAP his fingers in HALF!!"

"God, I was a drama king," Joe murmured. Ellie was going to get *such* a kick out of reading these. Still, their past self *had* been right about bras. "Yack," indeed. Joe's fingers absently tapped along their chest, safely smooshed down beneath their jacket and t-shirt by the binder Ellie had gotten them for their birthday.

Enough of that; they had work to do. Joe shut the notebook and tossed it back in with the others. Then they zipped open the suitcase, threw open the fabric lid in one fluid motion, revealing its interior — empty.

In went the shoebox of diaries. Then some of the old t-shirts, just for nostalgia's sake. Joe pulled out their phone and headed to the notes app — but not before they saw Ellie had texted them a minute ago: *"You got this, babe!!!"* followed by about ten thousand emojis.

"Thanks," they typed back, adding a heart. *"This might take longer than expected. Daddy made dinner."*

They watched the *"..."* as their girlfriend typed a response, taking small comfort just imagining Ellie's stout fingers with their chipped purple nail polish tapping out her response. *"That's fine. I'll wait however long you need."* A kissy face emoji and a whole parade of hearts followed.

Joe left the texting app and headed to the notes app. Then, using the list they'd put together to remind them what they needed, they moved around their childhood bedroom, grabbing stuff to add to the growing mess inside the suitcase. There really wasn't that much — most of the stuff they wanted to keep was already safe in the apartment they shared with Ellie and Gabe, just a few minutes from campus.

Last on the list: *rosaries*. Where had past Joe put those?...oh, right. They pulled open their old underwear drawer, which was mostly empty besides a few sad crumpled socks missing their match, plus a couple dust bunnies. But there in the corner was that coin purse they'd won in an elementary school fun fair, God, *so* many years ago. It was the round kind with the metal clasp at the top that you snap open and closed.

They snapped it open.

Peering in, they sort of felt like they'd just pried open an oyster to reveal a miraculous multitude of pearls. *And every pearl a prayer,* they thought, reaching fingers in to fish one out — the one with the purple glass beads they'd inherited from a great aunt they'd never met. As they pulled it out, two other rosaries tried to come with it, tangled together as they all were.

Sorry, Ma — I'll untangle those later. When I'm free of this place, Joe promised.

Snapping the little purse shut again and tucking it among the t-shirts filling half the suitcase, Joe reached into their jacket pocket once more. This time, when their fingers curled around the item inside, they pulled it out.

"This is it, huh Ma?" they said to the olive wood statuette in their palm. "Showtime."

The wooden figure didn't respond, obviously, but Joe always felt like those carved eyes had depth and warmth behind them —a window to the woman the figure represented.

Joe thought back to the day Gabe had pressed her into Joe's hand — *"Here. Based on that dream of yours."* He'd brushed off Joe's awe and fervent thanks — *"You know my process, dude. I can't hardly take credit. It's just what called out to me from the wood."* Gabe wasn't even a Christian — kinda hated Christianity's guts, which. Fair. He was agnostic, currently exploring paganism and witchcraft and literally anything *but* Christianity — yet he'd taken the time to whittle the Mother of God for a friend. For Joe.

Joe's thumb traced the folds of the wooden figure's robes. "You'll be with me for this, won't you, Ma?"

No voice had to reverberate from the heavens, let alone from a piece of wood, for Joe to know in the very core of their being what the answer was. *Yes, yes, forever yes.*

Tucking the statue of Mary back in their pocket, Joe zipped up their suitcase and pulled it from the bed — heavier now than it had been, but not too bad — and carried it to the door.

Down the stairs they went, taking care not to bang the bag against the walls. They deposited it right at the foot of the stairs, then made their way into the kitchen, where they could hear their parents bustling about. On the way, they took a moment to regard the Christmas tree in all its shining splendor: the neatly spaced ornaments, the glittering tinsel, and to top it all, the angel passed down across generations on their dad's side. Its white robes were somewhat yellowed with age, but it still managed to look majestic from its perch among pine branches. Joe imagined it was a good bit blonder than any angel who would have visited first-century Palestine. *Or maybe that's why all the angels had to open with "Be not afraid" — "Hey, I know I'm as pasty as some of the Romans oppressing your people but don't freak out…"*

But they were postponing the inevitable. It was time to face the music.

The first words out of their mom's mouth when they entered the kitchen were in chipper singsong: "Honey, hoo-ood!"

Oh, right. Bracing themself, Joe pulled their hood down.

Their mother's smile slipped from her face and shattered on the floor. Joe nearly expected her to clap her hands to her mouth like a movie character, so dramatic was her dismay. "Oh, Jen…it's as short as a man's!"

That's the point. "Yeah, listen —"

"Did the hairdresser mess it up? You know I tell you not to be frugal when it comes to haircuts, it's worth the extra money for a competent stylist —"

"No, Mom, I *asked* for this cut." Joe swallowed around the lump threatening to plug up their throat. "It's…" No no no, they *couldn't* do this. Not with Dad's hands as frozen as his expression, ladle midway between crock pot and half-filled bowls of chili. "…It's hipster." *Are you really channeling Mrs. Rudyard right now? Wow.*

Things thawed out; Joe's dad continued ladling chili and Joe's mom beckoned Joe to sit down at their usual place at the table.

"Y'know, I kind of like it," Dad said as he brought the first steaming bowl to the table and placed it in front of Joe. "It suits you." He reached out and ruffled the short hair. Joe only startled slightly, not enough for their parents to notice.

"Thanks, Daddy," they said, and halfway meant it. *Just wait till you know, till you really know…*

Joe said nothing more for the first few minutes of dinner, mindlessly moving their spoon from bowl to mouth as their mom filled them in on all the neighborhood gossip. They offered a grunt or "uh-huh" whenever Mom paused expectantly.

"Huh? Sorry, what?" Joe coughed, suddenly realizing both their parents were staring at them, as if waiting for something.

"I asked, do you know who *else* is back in town for Christmas, sweetie?" Mom said.

"Oh. Uh, no…"

"Jackson Everette! You remember him? You know I *always* said, and his mother *always* agreed, that the two of you would make the *sweetest* couple —"

"Mom." Joe's spoon clattering into their now nearly-empty bowl made them jump; they hadn't even noticed they'd dropped it. Their mom jumped, too, while their dad just raised his eyebrows. "Mom, Daddy, I need to talk to you."

"Mother, Father, I have something to share with you — the best news that has come to our people in generations. But I worry you will hear it as catastrophe."

Anna's hands stilled in her lap. "Tell it to us, Maryam, and if it is of God, we will rejoice with you." Yoachim remained silent, but he regarded his daughter carefully.

Maryam sat down beside her mother, drew her mother's hand to herself. "Listen. An angel of God came to me, and then the Spirit of God overshadowed me —"

"An angel of the Lord visited my daughter?" her father exclaimed, clapping his hands together and lifting

*his face heavenward. "Daughter, this is joyous news!
Blessed be the day of your birth, my girl! Blessed be the
Most High who blessed us with you!"*

*Her mother squeezed her hand, and joined her
husband's exaltation: "Blessed be the name of the Lord
who heard our prayers, who opened my womb in my old
age in order to bring us joy!"*

*Maryam's eyes shone as she returned Anna's
squeeze. "I so hoped you would understand!" she said.
"Blessed be the Spirit who defies expectation, who
opened my womb, that the lowliest of humankind might
bear the very son of God!"*

*"Amen, amen! I — what, my child?" Yoachim
moved his gaze from the ceiling to return it to his
daughter. "…Your womb?"*

"I need you to listen, really *listen*."

Dad cleared his throat and said, "Of course,
Jenny. We're listening."

"That's the first thing — I'm not that name
anymore. Jenny. Or Jennifer. Or Jen." Saying those
names felt like coughing up sharp rocks. "I'm…"
Their true name stuck in their throat. They couldn't,
they couldn't say it they couldn't say any of this
they —

Words from their dream rose up over the panic in their mind, washed over the chaos in soothing waves. *"To face the world's disgrace is to follow in my footsteps."* Then Ellie's voice, too: *"You got this, babe."*

Joe looked towards the Christmas tree again, to the angel at its peak. It regarded them with its vague expression: no judgment, no expectation. It simply bore witness, far beyond any pomp and circumstance so human as coming out. From its otherworldly vantage point, the momentous shrank down to the minor. No matter what happened in this kitchen, the world would keep turning; eon would slip into eon as unshaken angels watched.

Joe took a deep breath. Keeping their eyes on the angel's, they spoke: "My name is Joe, now. And I'm not a girl. The person I'm dating is, though. A girl, I mean. Or like…a woman. You know, like my age. A, uh, another college student." *Reeeeal eloquent, Joe. All that practicing in the mirror all week totally paid off.*

Joe forced themself to move their gaze to the two faces across from them. Their parents were staring with expressions so shocked that honestly, it would have been hilarious in any other situation.

As it was, Joe couldn't bear to keep seeing them, so they looked down at their bowl as they continued hurriedly, "And before you bring up religion I want you to know, I had this dream or like a vision thing where Mary told me it's okay — that being queer is okay and maybe even holy? So you don't have to be scared for my immortal soul or whatever, I'm still Christian and…yeah. God's chill with it. I think."

Silence screamed into the room and filled it full — silence that scraped like sandpaper across the ears. Joe kept staring into their bowl, too scared to look up at their parents. *Sorry, Ma. I'm not as brave as you.* They reached into their pocket again, gripping the carved figure inside as that sadistic silence stretched and scraped.

When Joe couldn't take it anymore, they spat a question into the remnants of their chili: "Well? Anyone gonna say something?"

Unable to repress the smile blooming across her lips, Maryam replied, "Father, Mother, the angel told me I'll give birth to the very son of God. And it's true — I am with child!"

Anna reacted first, her face crumpling like the heap of linen in her lap. "Who did this to you? Maryam, darling, did someone force himsel—"

"Mother, no!" Maryam shook her head so vehemently her ringlets shook against her cheeks. "It wasn't like that, I promise."

"Is it, is it Yosef's, then?" Anna's eyes took on a hopeful gleam. "Did the two of you sleep together already? You can tell us, that would be all right—"

"No, Mother, I told you — it was the Holy Spirit who came to me, no man at all!" Maryam closed her eyes for a moment, collected her thoughts. "I know that this is hard to understand; why, I asked the angel myself, 'How can I bear a child without knowing a man?' and the angel explained—" She was cut off not by a voice, but a thud. Her father had slammed his fist down on the table.

Maryam had never witnessed a violent action from her father, not once; he was a gentle, gentle man. She sank back into her seat as her mother pulled her hand away from hers.

"Maryam, how could you do this to me? To us?" Maryam dared a glance at Yoachim's face, and saw it was not hardened with rage, but melted into grief. His voice was something like keening as he moaned, "Oh my girl, my gift from God himself, why would you do this to your loving parents?"

Maryam stood, moved toward her father as he leaned into the wall, as if drained of all spirit — but he held up a hand to hold her back. She stood helplessly, longing to reach for him, to support him, to help him to a chair, anything! But it was as if a chasm had opened in the floor between them. "Father, please believe me, there was no man!"

"Then what makes you think there is a pregnancy?" Anna's voice came from behind her, suddenly businesslike. She had stood from her sewing, letting it fall to the floor, to approach her daughter and press her hands to Maryam's stomach.

"I've had no monthly cycle. And, well…" How did she explain that she simply felt what was growing inside her — had since the day of the Spirit? She knew that was not how pregnancy worked, that the quickening did not come for several months. Yet though the Presence inside her did not move, it could not be denied. A warmth glowed in her belly night and day, like a flame that did not burn.

"My darling, darling girl," Yoachim continued from his wall, "you have never brought us heartache, not since *the day God answered our prayers! Must all our joy be twisted into grief?"*

Maryam couldn't think of a tactful way to say "This isn't about you," nor did she think her father expected an answer anyway. She kept silent.

"Does Yosef know?" Anna asked cautiously, and that spark of hope had returned to her eyes — but it flickered out as soon as Maryam answered,

"Yes, Mother. I told him last week."

"Oh, my silly, naïve girl!" she cried; but there was no malice in it, only despair. She began to pace in the small space between her daughter and the bench. "What did he say?"

"He said he'll come talk to Father soon — that he will end our contract, but seek no penalty or restitution."

Anna threw up her hands. "Well! I suppose we must thank him for his generosity!" she exclaimed, sarcasm dripping. "He could ruin us, but no, he's only sentencing you to a life of shame!"

"It is generous of him," Yoachim spoke up, addressing Anna instead of the wall at last. "He could have our girl stoned, if he insisted. A good man," he

added, and his voice grew distant again. "A good, good man…he would have made a perfect son-in-law."

"Father, I do not need Yosef!" Maryam insisted. Not that it hadn't been a dagger in her heart when he told her they were done — that he did not believe her story, that he would not help her raise this holy child. But in spite of that, she believed what she said next as firmly as she believed anything: "Beloved Father, I do not need even you, or any man. God will let no harm come to me, with this child in my womb!"

"Silly girl!" Anna cried again, and now she did seem angry. "God does not work like that, and you know it; we raised you better! The way things are, we women need a man to protect us — and God knows your father and I both have only so many years left in this world!"

Yoachim responded to that: "Oh, God most high! What is to become of my daughter, my only child, when I am dead and in my grave? Oh!" And he began to wail.

Maryam could take no more. To have her joy, her celebration, received as grief by the ones she loved most — it was too much. She fled her home, leaving the noise of her father's grief behind.

The wind's bite felt like kindness on Joe's overheated cheeks as they hurried down the now-dark street, their suitcase's wheels keeping rhythm with their pace. They passed the Rudyards' inflatable Nativity, with its pasty white Mary and Joseph beaming down at pink-cheeked baby Jesus. They passed the Longs' unkempt yard, its dead leaves and toy guns. At last, there was Ellie's car, the trans-flag-backed "T4T" and vivid rainbow "honk if you're gay" bumper stickers sticking out like sore thumbs in this prim cis-hetero haven. Joe made for it like an oasis in the desert.

In the driver's seat, which was tilted back as far as it could go, Ellie was completely zonked out. A little rivulet of drool meandered down her chin from her open mouth. Some of the roiling in Joe's gut calmed at the sight. They knocked gently at the window, and Ellie jolted awake, eyes snapping open and mouth snapping shut. Even through the closed window, Joe could read Ellie's lips saying "I'm up!"

Joe gave a little wave, and pointed back towards the trunk. Ellie's fingers fumbled around on the dash for a moment; then the trunk popped open.

"Hey, baby," Ellie said after Joe had let themself in the passenger-side door and collapsed into the seat. Her voice had that gravely timber it always had just after waking up, but she was clearly trying to act like she wasn't groggy at all. "How'd it go?" She reached a hand over and rubbed Joe's shoulder; Joe leaned into the touch as they tried to decide how to answer.

Their mom's voice, hurt and upset and increasingly frantic, blared unbidden through their mind. *"Did someone at school hurt you? Is it something we did? You were such a happy little girl..."* *"Why did you have to do this* now? *Couldn't you have kept it to yourself, so we could enjoy Christmas together?"* Their father's face also flashed through their mind, and for a moment, Joe thought they were going to be sick. He had just *sat* there, eyes staring at nothing the whole time, as silent as the angel topping the tree a few feet behind him. Joe had anticipated most of their mom's comments. But Dad's utter silence? They had not expected it, and somehow it was worse than any words he could have flung at them. He hadn't even looked up when Joe finally pushed their chair back from the table and left.

"Can we talk about it later?" they finally said, swiping a hand over their eyes. "I just wanna get out of here right now."

"Sure, love."

They had one last destination before they could finally leave this godawful suburb behind. Ellie already knew it, so she and Joe both stayed quiet for the ten or so minutes it took to get to Our Lady of the Wayside Catholic Church, Ellie's right hand gripping Joe's left the whole time.

As Ellie pulled the keys from the ignition, Joe suddenly blurted, "It just sucks! It sucks, because like…figuring out I'm queer, that I'm *in love*, that I'm the happiest I've ever been in my *life*…I wanted to share all that with them, you know? But to them, it's the end of the damn world."

Ellie reached across the console and pulled her partner as close as possible while in a car. "I know, baby. I know," she murmured softly, stroking Joe's hair. Before Joe knew it, they were crying, then sobbing, right there in the parking lot of Joe's childhood church. Ellie let them cry for Joe didn't even know how long, periodically murmuring little phrases like "That's right, just let it out."

By the time Joe had wrung every last tear from their eyes, they had thoroughly soaked their girlfriend's shoulder. "Sorry about that," they said, voice a little stuffy.

"It's fine, babe. It's all fine." Ellie moved a strand of hair from Joe's wet eyes. "You ready now?"

"Yeah."

Ellie grabbed her cane from the back seat before they started the trek across the parking lot. Joe took Ellie's free hand, and let the rhythm of their girlfriend's mobility aid, its sturdy *tap* sounding forth with every other step, soothe them into a steadier state of mind. The straight white lines of empty parking spaces glowed faintly, and Joe imagined that, to the watchful gaze of the lampposts towering above, they and Ellie were glowing, too.

When they reached the several steps that led up to three sets of tall arched doors, Joe said, "Wait here" before ascending them on their own — no use making Ellie climb stairs if she didn't have to. As Joe suspected, the doors all turned out to be "Locked…locked…aaaaand locked." They hopped back down to where their girlfriend waited.

"No worries," Joe said. "The inside wasn't the main event, anyway. Follow me."

Ellie shrugged and followed after Joe, who led the way around the building till they came to a gap in the brick. A short corridor later, they came into a small courtyard swathed in shadow, the only light a small ground spotlight and the sliver of moon — waning crescent, Joe was pretty sure — that had reached its zenith as they drove.

At the center of the courtyard's couple of benches and well-groomed shrubbery was a life-sized statue. The ground light tilted to peer up at this statue, its feeble gold beam splashing across the speckled gray stone.

As Ellie sat down on one of the benches, Joe approached the stone figure. They paused to gaze up into its softly illuminated face, which bore simple features: lips that curved into a gentle smile; nose; hint of downturned eyes beneath their lids and brow. The artist had carved flowing robes across the shoulders, the outstretched arms, the belted waist, as well as a veil covering the head — all typical for a statue of the Mother of God.

Joe settled themself down at the statue's feet. They were aware of their girlfriend's eyes on them, and for a moment, anxiety rippled across their gut — Joe knew what she thought about the Catholic penchant for statues and icons and Saints and crosses…but Joe let the feeling go. They reminded themself that Ellie loved them, didn't judge them, respected that their ways of expressing faith differed. They returned their focus to the statue's face, now several feet above them.

"Hey, Ma," they said quietly. "Just wanted to say goodbye to this particular statue of you. …Wait, that's probably weird." *Or like, idolatry or something.*

It was this courtyard in general they had wanted to visit, one last time. Back in middle and high school, Joe had poured out so much angst into this little corner of their home church's grounds…had murmured or shouted so many prayers in here that surely *some* ghost of them lingered among the shrubbery branches, in the stone folds of Mary's robes.

Joe thought back to that afternoon from five years back, when they had fallen at the feet of this very statue and cried like a baby, *finally* admitting to themself that they liked girls. The quiet gray stone had taken it all. The serene expression had not twisted in disgust. At that time, Joe still believed queerness was sin, or sickness, or *something,* but after that day, they at least knew it wasn't "bad enough" to cause the ground at Mary's feet to swallow them straight down into hell, or Communion wafers to scorch their tongue.

And then, just a year ago, the dream had come — not here in this courtyard, but all the way over at their college church. Joe's lips turned up at the corners, and they absentmindedly fiddled with the zipper on their jacket pocket as they reminisced…

They'd signed up for the 3am shift of Adoration because hey, they were hardly sleeping anyway back then. Plus, the idea of an hour alone with God without having to worry about anyone barging in was an appealing one. They could really use some guidance because, *God,* they were scared. They were petrified their life was spiraling out of their control, leading them where God would not, could not follow.

They had relieved the previous volunteer of their duty a few minutes before, right as the clock struck three, and the sanctuary was stiller than a tomb. From their kneeling position in a front row pew, Joe gazed, mesmerized, at the monstrance glittering golden in the candlelight up on the altar. Inside the circle of glass at its heart, the round wafer that *was,* Church teaching said, *the* Body of Christ sat pale and still.

Eventually, Joe moved their eyes from that pale circle in its scintillating frame long enough to fish their rosary from their backpack. As they did, their fingers brushed against a folded piece of paper with a lipstick kiss stamped across its white surface. *Ugh, don't think about that.* Or maybe…do? Bring it to God and ask for — for what? Forgiveness? Acceptance? Joe didn't know! They just did not know, and the uncertainty was ripping their spirit to shreds.

Fingers trembling a little, they draped their rosary over one hand, held the first bead between two fingers of the other. They began to pray, murmuring the Apostle's creed, and then the "Our Father," and then the "Hail Mary" again and again as their fingers moved from bead to bead. The repetition of the words they knew better than any others, accompanied by the quiet clinking of the beads, eventually lulled them into that blissful state where thoughts drifted away. There was only the bead between their fingertips, the prayer on their lips, the flickering of candles up ahead…

And then, there was Mary.

She stood between Joe and the altar — in front of, but not blocking the host behind her — and her brown skin glowed, not with the candlelight but with an inward radiance.

"Look at you. Look at you! My beautiful one!" Her voice filled Joe's entire being up, warming them from the tips of their toes to the top of their head. Joe gaped up at her from their pew, for how long, they couldn't say. Then abruptly, bashfulness enveloped them, and they looked downward, towards the string of beads now slack in their hands.

"My...my Lady," they stuttered, unsure how to address this apparition.

"My child," Mary replied, and Joe's cheeks blushed hot as they felt a palm cup their chin and gently raise their face upward again. "My child. Enough of this fear and shame. Do you not know that Divinity pulses through your cells, as surely as it nestled in my womb?"

"I..." Joe had no idea what to say to that. They had longed for, begged for a sign like this — and now that it had come, they could barely believe it. "Are you saying...are you saying I'm okay? Me and all this gender mess, and, and me and Ellie..." They trailed off, and could not help but look away again.

"*Yes*." The answer reverberated through Joe's bones. "Yes, yes, forever yes." Joe dared to raise their gaze again, to lose themself in the deep brown universe of Mary's eyes. "My child. Be bold! To face the world's disgrace is to follow in my footsteps."

Then, before they could respond to *that* incredible statement, before they could break down in thanks and reverence, the four o'clock volunteer had shaken them awake, holding up the rosary that had tumbled to the floor when Joe slumped in their pew.

Maybe it *had* been a dream — but at the same time, Joe knew it had been more than a dream, too. It had sewn their shredded spirit back together, emboldened them for what they had to do.

Now, it was done. It had gone more or less how they'd known it would, and *God*, it hurt — but now, here in this courtyard, they let relief wash over them. Everything was out in the open now. The ball was in their parents' court — they could puncture it if they wanted, even build a wall where now there was just a net. Joe had done their part and was free, either way; they were whole, and they were loved, either way.

She hadn't gotten more than ten feet from her own front door before she heard her own name called — but while the voice was familiar, it belonged to neither of her parents. "…Yosef?"

The man approaching her seemed out of breath, and his hair was tousled as if from sleep. "Maryam! I am so glad to see you — I have come to —"

"Inform my father of the divorce. I know." Maryam was rarely brusque with anyone, but seeing Yosef again, after what just took place…it was too much.

"No! Maryam, no. I — wait. Forgive me, I know it is inappropriate to speak here, like this. But if you will have the grace to listen, I would beg your mercy."

"My…my mercy?" Maryam's head felt light. "I don't understand."

"You shared your situation with me, and I reacted hastily. Listen, I had this dream, and — well, I can explain all that later. For now…" Yosef paused. He ran a hand through his rumpled hair. Up to this point, he had kept his eyes downcast — out of respect or disdain, Maryam had not been sure — but now, he raised them and met hers. "I would ask you to take me back. To be my wife, and let me be your husband, and be the father of this child of yours. If you would have me."

Maryam's mouth opened. "I have only one question."

"Anything."

"Do you believe me? Do you believe what I told you happened?"

Yosef's gaze did not waver. "I do."

"Feels good to be on the road again!" Ellie said as she pressed down on the gas and merged onto the interstate. "I'm telling you, you're going to *love* my dads, and they're gonna love you. This is a spoiler and I don't think I'm supposed to tell you, but they even bought some stockings for the fireplace, so they can give you a little taste of Christmas."

"Dang, that's…that's really sweet of them," Joe said, touched. "They didn't have to do that just for me."

"Yeah well, that's the kind of people they are," Ellie shrugged. Then she joked, "I think your stocking has Santa or whatever on it, but *mine* has a *dreidel* so no one will get any ideas about us being a Christian family now. …I don't even know where they managed to *find* a Jewish stocking; the world truly is an astonishing place…"

Ellie's voice faded from Joe's hearing – not because she'd stopped talking, but because Joe had just checked their phone, and the notifications brightening the screen seemed impossible; they expanded and filled Joe's entire brain, muffling all outside sound and scenery.

Two missed calls. One voicemail. All from Dad.

"H-hey," they finally managed to say, holding up one hand, "c-can you pause a minute? I gotta…"

Ellie quieted, and Joe clicked *play* on the voicemail.

"Hey, Jen—shoot, I'm sorry. Sorry. Joe? Honey. Hey. I'm so sorry about, well, about freezing up and just sitting there while your mom did all the talking. I was just shocked – no, that's not what I wanted to say. It's not like there weren't clues…no, wait. That's not it, either. What I wanted to say was that I…I might not be one hundred percent on board with everything you told us, but the thought of losing you…" the voice broke, paused a long, long moment. "Listen, can we try again? Please, don't leave town just yet. Maybe we can talk a little more. Call me back — or text if you want, I know kids these days don't do phone calls. Or if you don't wanna talk just yet, I get that, too. Just…just know your daddy still loves you, no matter what." A *click* signaled the recording's end. Then there was silence, except for the muted sounds of tires on concrete and wind rushing by outside the car.

"Joe?" Ellie finally said. "Was that your dad?"

They cleared their throat. "Yeah, it was," they said. "Hey, can we stop for the night? Instead of going straight to your house."

"On it." Ellie merged into the rightmost lane. "I'll take the next exit. We can get a motel room." Ellie was good like that. God, Joe loved her.

"You are literally the best," Joe said.

"I know."

"I love you so much."

"I know," Ellie said with a grin, keeping her eyes on the road.

And then they both were quiet again. With shaky fingers, Joe opened their texting app and started to type.

"Want to get breakfast at 9? IHOP or something?"

The ellipses showing their dad was texting back popped up almost before Joe hit *send*. They waited. *"Yes. Thank u, Jo."*

Joe's throat felt closed up once again, but weirdly in a good way. *"It's Joe with an e,"* they typed back. *"See you then"*

"Joe. See u tomorrow." Pause, then another text. *"Whats her name?"*

Joe huffed. "What?" Ellie asked.

"He asked, 'What's her name?' I assume he means you, but doesn't want to call you my girlfriend or something?"

Ellie snorted. "Ah well, give it time." She glanced from the road ahead long enough to smile softly at her partner. "Honestly, this is incredible, Joe."

"Yeah. I...he's even calling me Joe. I never thought that would happen." Not after the comments they'd heard their parents make when transgender stuff popped up in the news. Not after years of witnessing them nod along when gay people came up in Sunday homilies. Joe's hand wandered to their pocket, wrapped around the wood figure inside. They hesitated, then added, "It feels like a miracle."

"You never know!" Ellie replied. "You do have that nice blue lady in the sky looking out for you, right?"

Joe punched their girlfriend's arm lightly. "Shut up."

"Nah, Joe, I mean it," Ellie said, glancing Joe's way again to make sure they could tell she was serious. "Look, *I* don't believe in her or whatever, but I *do* believe in you, babe. I believe you when you say that dream of yours had some kind of meaning. And I'm glad — I like thinking that God or *some* sort of supernatural entity is looking out for my lover in ways I can't."

Warmth blossomed from somewhere in Joe's very core. "Thanks, El. That means a lot."

Ellie just smiled softly, and the car got quiet again. Joe returned to their phone, texted back one last time: *"My girlfriend's name is Ellie, and she's the best."*

Pause. *"Got it. Love u."*

"Love you too, daddy."

Joe stared at the messages till their screen went dark. Then, they looked up and out the windshield, just as Ellie was turning into a motel. It was a dingy looking place, and the "O" in the flickering pink neon sign was completely dark. But to Joe in that moment, it could have been a luxury resort.

One hand squeezed the wooden figure of Mary in their pocket. The other reached for their girlfriend's right hand where it rested on the gearshift. Ellie turned to look at them, and her smile glowed brighter than the motel's neon.

As they crossed their second parking lot of the evening, this one stippled with cars, Ellie threw her head back to admire the sky, stippled with stars that even all the light pollution could not blot out.

"Waxing crescent! My favorite phase," she said, pointing moonward with her chin since one hand was occupied with her cane, the other with a duffel.

"One, I *adore* that you have a favorite moon phase," Joe grinned; "two, I thought that was a *waning* crescent?"

"Nah, the moon grows light from the right — it's definitely growing out of new right now, not into new."

Joe studied the thin sliver of white bordering the right side of the black sphere, darker than the black surrounding it. "Ohhh. Thanks for the astronomy lesson, babe." They smiled up at it. "Y'know, I think that's my favorite phase, too."

Ellie gasped theatrically. "Stealing my favorite moon phase? Get your own!"

They were both giggling as they approached the check-in counter. While Ellie talked to the tired-looking employee behind the desk, Joe took a moment to savor their wonder at how a day they'd been dreading for weeks, if not years, was ending with them joking and laughing with the girl they loved. *You really* do *have something to do with this, don't you, Ma? I know how you love an upending of expectations.*

An hour later found them in a grubby motel bed, nestled together cozy as mice in a burrow. Joe snored softly, dreaming of rosaries beaded with full, bright moons, of angels with pink neon haloes, of Communion hosts honeyed with hope, as Ellie held them warm and safe in her arms.

Author's Note

Mary has been in my corner all my life, nudging me gently but firmly towards deeper understandings of what it means to follow her queer Son. Telling this fictional story about Joe's encounter with the Mother of God let me express some of my own feelings about Mary, whom I have come to see as a patron Saint of queer and particularly trans folk.

As a child, I mostly fell for depictions of Mary the sweet and submissive, meek and mild. And certainly, she *does* identify herself as God's servant — but hers is not a passive submission, an unquestioning obedience. Moreover, the Catholic Church of my youth raised Mary on a pedestal of perfect purity, skipping over the fact that the people of her own day likely saw her as sexually "indecent!" In this way, Mary's own experiences with disgrace, and her defiance in the face of social norms, resonate with many LGBTQA+ narratives.

We only get glimpses of Mary throughout the Gospels, but these glimpses combine into an image of a woman with guts, a woman with things to say, unafraid of impropriety and eager for empire's end. The Nativity story we retell each Advent season depicts a girl who dares ask questions of a divine messenger ("How can this be, since I have not known a man?"), making sure she has all the details *before* agreeing with that angel's message ("Let it happen to me according to your word"); who exclaims her joy that through God, the pregnancy the world calls shameful will come to be praised across the ages (see Luke 1). Fast forwarding several decades, John 2's story of the Wedding at Cana depicts a mother telling her adult son what to do, in a culture where adult sons had legal authority over their mothers. Even when Jesus hesitates, Mary *believes* in his ability to fill a need they both observe, and she helps him kickstart his ministry with the miracle of a rollicking good party. Years later, when most of Jesus's male followers flee in fear of legal consequences, Mary stands steadfast at the foot of her son's cross (John 19); after his Ascension into heaven, she becomes a beloved matriarch among his apostles (Acts 1).

Then there are the various apparitions of Mary that, according to Catholic tradition, have taken place over the centuries, all across the world. Almost always, Mary appears to persons whom society overlooks or even despises, including: Bernadette, a poor and sickly French shepherdess; Adele Brise, a young Belgian immigrant in Wisconsin; 18th century Vietnamese villagers hiding out from their persecutors in the jungle; and my personal favorite, Juan Diego, a Chichimec peasant in Mexico.

Venerated as Our Lady of Guadalupe, Mary appeared to Juan Diego several times in December

1531 with instructions to build a shrine on the hill where he saw her. From this shrine, she told him, she would extend her mercy and protection to "all the inhabitants on this land and all the rest who love me, invoke and confide in me; listen there to their lamentations, and remedy all their miseries, afflictions and sorrows" (from the English translation of the *Nican Mopoha*). However, the Spanish Bishop to whom Juan Diego relayed this request refused to believe this Indigenous peasant without proof — after all, why would the Mother of God, Queen of Heaven, deign to appear to a lowly "Indian"? Mary provided that proof in the form of roses blooming out of season and her own image imprinted on Juan Diego's *tilma*, or cloak. To this day, around 15 million pilgrims visit the chapel where this *tilma* is displayed every single year.

What I love most about Our Lady of Guadalupe is that she appeared to Juan Diego not in the garb of the Spanish colonizers but in symbolically rich Aztec apparel, and with brown skin and dark hair. What is more, she spoke to him in his native Nahuatl, a language deemed barbaric and contemptible by the Spanish settlers. Mary the Palestinian Jew who lived under Roman occupation extended her solidarity to the Indigenous peoples who likewise endured oppression. She called Juan Diego by the loving diminutive "Juanito, Juan Dieguito," and declared herself his Mother.

After facing the bishop's disbelief, Juan Diego implored Mary to "entrust the delivery of your message to someone of importance, well known, respected, and esteemed, so that they may believe in him; because I am a nobody, I am a small rope, a tiny ladder, the tail end, a leaf…" Juan Diego knew that in the eyes of the world, he was worthless; perhaps he internalized that idea and even believed it about himself. But Mary's response makes clear her preference for the "nobodies" of the world, and affirms Juan Diego's dignity and worth: "Hark, my son the least, you must understand that I have many servants and messengers…but it is of precise detail that you yourself solicit and assist, and that through your mediation my wish be complied." Mary insists that it *must* be this Chichimec peasant, denigrated and overlooked, who carries her message — no one else will do.

This Mary — Mary the Defiant, Mary the Outspoken, Mary of the Oppressed and Overlooked — is the Mary who has mothered me through times of complacency *and* turmoil. She has challenged me when my thoughts have mirrored the status quo; she has let me cry on her shoulder when the status quo threatened to smother me.

When I was first discovering my own queerness, before I felt confident enough to bring my discoveries to the God who made me that way in the first place, it was to Mary that I turned. Her rejection would have shattered me — but as a traditional Catholic prayer, the *Memorare*, says of Mary: "Never was it known that anyone who fled to thy protection, implored thy help, or sought thine intercession was left unaided." Mary gathered me up and showed me how my queerness does not cut me off from her *or* the God she bore and nursed and raised. Both Mary and her Son identify so intimately with those whom the world hates that they count themselves as one of us — that includes us queer folk. Thus my queerness actually provides me with a unique connection to my Mother Mary and her Son, my God.

I have written many poems about Mary, particularly how she has given me encouragement and strength as I've learned how to bring my queerness into my faith. Some of them can be found in my published book of poetry, *The Kin-dom in the Rubble*; others in an episode of my *Blessed Are the Binary Breakers Podcast*: episode 32, "A Queer Nativity: God's Trans-ition, Mary's trans-gressive yes, and Joseph's trans-formation into an ally." I share two of the poems, both of which helped inspire my story about Joe, in the following pages.

Mary, Mother of us, your transgender children

The angel said to her, "Do not be afraid, Mary, for you have found favor with God. And now, you will conceive in your womb and bear a son. ...
Then Mary said, "Here am I, the servant of the Lord; let it be with me according to your word."
– Luke 1:28-38

This is a story of Mary consenting to enter into a disreputable condition, trusting that despite all appearances she is entering into holiness.[7]

you said Yes
to stoning.

you said Yes
to your mother seizing you by the wrists, yelling into your face
demanding to know *who did this to you* — to your father
weeping as you had never seen him weep, asking what he had done

---

[7] Excerpt from <u>Out in Scripture:</u> An honest encounter between LGBT lives & the Bible

that you would turn out like this, that you would
do this to him.

Mary, teenage girl with the unplumbed brown
eyes
Mary, hailed full of grace by a heavenly being
you said Yes to disgrace, to excommunication,
to childhood friends abandoning you, to the
isolation
of no "decent person" daring to associate with
you.

and as your body transformed in wondrous ways
—
God's feet forming, kicking, making
a rich round hill of your stomach,
God dependent, sustained by naught but a flimsy
cord
connecting Them to you,
God! growing, *becoming* in the darkness
of *your* womb!

— most did not celebrate with you.
your joy grew as your body changed,
and their snide comments, harsh stares
could not pierce your euphoria

— except for sometimes, when they did.
and for those sometimes,
when the rejection was too much, when
you crumpled at your bedside
weeping, shouting to God and whispering to
Them
begging to know why your neighbors' hearts are
so hard,
why your father cannot be moved to share your
joy,

my heart aches with its fullness of empathy for
you
and you for me – empathy sharp as a sword
or maybe a needle: pricking, piercing,
and stitching back into wholeness –

so that when i came to you on my knees that night
sorrowful and scared and *begging* you to be
my Mother still, begging you not to disown
your queer little not-girl,

you bent down and picked me up, your soft
strong arms
shielding me from the world's stares, your soft
calloused hands
loosening the rope around my neck, and you
whispered

soft and fierce, *I am your Mother, I am*
Mother to all like you, and I will not let any
who run to me be destroyed.

Queer Mother! – a motherhood thicker than
blood, deeper than the waters of the womb,
a relationship fashioned by a shared Yes
to disgrace, a fervent Yes
to the hard but healing path to holiness –

Mama, my Mama, i run always to you
and you give me the strength to shout with all my
might
God! let it be done to me according to your word!
transform me.

"Virgin" Mary, teen mom

Mary, teen mom,
in those uncertain days

between your jubilant "Yes!" to God seeking
shelter in you
and Joseph's "yes" to marrying you
despite your indiscretion (*daring* to get knocked
up out of wedlock!
Did childhood friends desert you? Did your father
weep in shame?)

would you have laughed, disbelieving, if informed
that the primary epithet bestowed on you
by those future generations who call you
blessed…
is *Virgin?*

Mary, teen mom, against whom every packed inn
turned its back,
about whom, maybe, neighbors laughed
and mothers told their daughters, "Don't be
like *her*"
(spitting your name like a nasty thing)…

you relate to the round-bellied girl
eating alone in a cafeteria crammed with cruel
stares;
you relate to the girl singled out at church
for wearing a "too-short" skirt,
blamed for the lust of grown men
who ought to pluck out their eyes for looking at
her at all!

…yet the words fastened to people like these are
much less pretty
than what *you* are called.

Mary, teenage rebel! –
you who embraced impropriety with a song

you, full of grace but called disgraceful
by men who would have you stoned –

what in heaven's name
does *virginity* have to do
with *you*?

…unless for you, virginity means
not "no" to sex
but "yes" to choosing for yourself,
defining yourself, controlling your own body,
your own life.

Hail, you
who looked the status quo
square in the eye – and laughed!

Hail, you
who saw the Grace in being called disgraceful
by a world not ready to be turned on its head.

Hail, you who defy categorization:
virgin or slut,
child of God or God's own mother,
obedient servant or the one who knew
Jesus would do all you told him to do
(and thus you brought fine wine
into a world that's parched for it)…

Teach us *this* defiance, devout rebel!
Teach us your fervor for God's revolution,
your thirst for liberation from convention.

The Birth of a Family
Luke 2:8-20
by Ha Na Park

Have you ever listened to the birth stories your family members tell? Or maybe you have told them yourself…

My children like to hear their birth stories: how they were born and what happened before and on the day of their arrival. My two sons were born at home. My older son Peace was laid on my bosom right after his birth on the warm bedroom floor (Not all Koreans sleep in beds.) My younger son Jah-bi was born "in the bathtub" at the lovely blue house we first rented on Vancouver Island; That's the way I tell the boys about their births. Then, Peace, who was 4 years old when his "little baby brother" was born, and my partner don't even wait to chime in and tell their parts, … *in detail* (You know what I mean!). But as the mother, what I often like to highlight is the moment of amazing mystery of the first eye contact I made with my children. The moment that tired baby Peace, about to cry, was laid on my chest, he opened just one eye with effort, just halfway, and when our eyes met, it seemed that he knew where he was and then he did not cry.

Adoption stories are often very powerful and moving, too. The families carefully weave together their own birth story through experience and memories: the story of how they first met, when and where, their first moments of the mysterious and powerful feeling of an immediate deep connection. By sharing the stories each year, or any time when the family wants to, the parents and children honour the birthday of their incredible love as a family.

Birth stories are often extremely powerful. They can immediately bring us back to a joyous moment, they can sadly remind us of some couple's struggles with infertility, they can stir our imaginations with children hoped for, and they can make us aware of the difficult circumstances some people had to overcome in their lives.

Birth stories are charged with deep emotion.

Ask any parent or grandparent or aunt or uncle, and of course, older siblings about the birth of a new baby (or the welcoming of a child to the family), and they typically can describe the event in great detail (Karyn Wiseman). As most birth stories begin, the storyteller sets the stage... They describe the setting and the situation into which the child was born. They bring us into the realities of the event. In the Gospels, we are told of the reasons the family travelled so late in Mary's pregnancy. We are brought into the place of the birth and why the location of his birth came about. The power of Jesus' birth story lies in its humbleness - - a babe born in a stable, wrapped in simple cloth, and laid to rest in an animal trough. It is the reality that reflects/represents so many birth stories in the world. It's the story of real poverty. It's the story of marginalization. It's the story of many refugees and immigrants. It's the story of the babies, the children of God, whose family can't find accommodation, haven't received the generosity, kindness and acceptance of society... *if we only look at the stable scenes, the manger scenes, the humbleness or the dire situation that Mary and Joseph suffer or embrace...*

And yet, in today's Gospel, all of a sudden, the others begin to chime in to not lose any time to tell their parts and to weave the whole of the story together...

First, the shepherds came in a hurry, and they told their story to Mary and Joseph with great joy. (Indeed, we are told that "Thus is born the true saviour of the world - not Caesar Augustus, the oppressor, the colonizer, the false saviour of the world, the protector of those with power and privilege, but Christ the Lord, whose birth is 'good news of great joy for all the people.'" Shepherds tell

143

the story: "Mary, Joseph. We are the shepherds living in the fields near here. As you know, our job is just the same, every day. We keep watch over our flock by day and by night. But tonight was different. Just before we came to you, Oh My Lord, we were terrified. We were not sure what we were seeing at first, but an ANGEL of the Lord appeared and stood before us! You should have seen the glory of God. The light, … the beautiful light shone and surrounded us. We were frozen in the moment, terrified, and curious. We didn't have time to ask each other, What's going on? Can you believe this? We just couldn't turn our eyes away. Then the angel spoke to US. The Angel's voice was so soft, tender and kind, and the Angel said, 'Do not be afraid; See — I am bringing you good news of great joy for all the people. … This will be a sign for you: You will find a child wrapped in bands of cloth and lying in a manger.' AND THERE WERE SO MANY ANGELS – a whole heavenly choir, and they sang, 'Glory to God in the highest heaven, and on earth peace among those whom God favours'. So the angel told us to come here and tell you this and see the baby, and when an angel tells you to do something, you HAVE to do it, right? This baby is special – wait, what's his name? Jesus is God's child, and a blessing for you and for us, the whole entire world… Never doubt that." The Bible tells us, "All who heard it were amazed at what the shepherds told them. But Mary treasured all these words and pondered them in her heart."

Maybe the thing about remembering the birth of a baby and telling the story is that everyone has their memories and they are all different. We are all natural meaning-makers, story-tellers, connecting what we see and hear with our own life situations, identity, hopes…, drawing lines between the dots - which have sometimes been laid aside, neglected and forgotten - and adding colours to the event to celebrate and experience again and again when the stories are shared with more people and in more places.

Count the actors in the Nativity stories. Shepherds. Mary. Joseph. The Angel. The Magi. The Innkeepers. Even King Herod… The narrative becomes more complex, richer - just like any family's life becomes richer and more complex with the birth of a child…

The mystery of Christmas is that somehow we all can relate ourselves to the story of a baby wrapped in simple cloth and laid in a manger. It offers an entry point into our life's and world's complexities. It is, after all, the birth story of all birth stories *and it's a story of family.* For many people, Christmas is both an exciting and a stressful time. Some families struggle with overwhelming burdens of care. For others, memories of closeness are accompanied by memories of loss and grief. Christmas is a space which invites the coming together of many significant life issues - experiences, often unexamined or unarticulated... Perhaps that's when the stories of the birth of the holy child makes connection to the weary, tired part of our lives: We need the angels, the romance, the starlight, the symbols and the colour of the story. We can enter the story, find ourselves there, make our own exploratory journeys with the shepherds, just to see, to be there, and tell our part of the whole of the story... Then, and there, God joins the family... The Starlight falls down to the earth, "spreads diamonds" to the hearts of those who await hope and good news at midnight, rather than just watching over the earth and its people. God joins the family with both its fragility and strength, trading the freedom of power and distance to join us. God, out of all the judgements God has wielded, God chooses to "sacrifice" judgement and become vulnerable in order to fully exist with us, in the story of the humble birth of hope, and make permanent connection with us. And this story of the birth of the holy child is told generation to generation, place to place, all the time, every year.

Concluding this message, I believe it is quite a relevant and true blessing to share the reflection of Stan McKay (Newsletter, Dec 2019, of Sandy-Saulteaux Spiritual Centre): The Birth of a Child.

"In my home on Fisher River First Nation, we have celebrated Christmas for many generations. We understand the importance of the birth of a child as a sign of hope and new beginnings. We are discussing ceremonies for celebrating with families whenever a baby is born. In our cultural understanding, we know that every time a child is born there is a renewed hope for the future of our community."

This Christmas, how about telling the stories of a birth of a child, a baby, a family's love, a new hope in your family? Joy, hope for healing, accompanies us when we tell our stories of new birth, in wonder, beauty, kindness and friendship...

on traditional biblical family values (a nativity)
by Johanna E. H.

I bring you a strange scene, to be sure:

the woman— or rather, girl—
scrawny, panting, eyes bright,
bared for the first time before her husband,
full of holy terror
("Do not be afraid" still ringing in her ears,
command unheeded),
a king crowning
between her legs,
her cries disturbing the guests at the inn;

the man, older, still awkward around his new
wife,
unused to being around this, unprepared
for the blood and screaming,
hands messy and brow furrowed,
robe torn for his firstborn son to be wrapped in;

the angel,
androgynous and unseen in the rafters,
sympathetic but unable to relate to the
pain, the messiness
of humanity,
unsure how their God will use this moment,

but feeling Them all the same;

and the child,
taking his first gasping breaths,
taking in the cold room,
the crying (even the angel lets a tear slip),
and he has wide brown eyes (taking after his
mother—
who else?)
and beautiful little hands,
blood-covered, an omen if you squint;

and then there's the ass and the ox,
and their hay and shit and noise;

and at first you might not know what
family values
I am giving you with this image,
but look closer.
Look at the love—
you can almost see it in the musty air.
I'm bringing you the first Christian family,
queer and dirty and trusting.

And I see them all around me,
in queer families and unhoused families
and refugee families
and every family full of

tangible love and/or loneliness
and strange scenes.

My values
are here, in this barn,
in the little brown boy with bloody hands and
light in his eyes, just like his mother and Father.

Comfort and Joy
by Neil Ellis Orts

A few days ago, I heard, as you do this time of year, "God Rest Ye Merry Gentlemen" in passing. I don't think I was even paying much attention to it. It was just part of the season's soundscape.

And that's when something can hit you unexpectedly. This year, this time, the phrase "comfort and joy" caught my attention. More precisely, the word "comfort" caught me.

I can't tell you exactly why it hit, what my emotional state of the moment was. I can say that I've had a bit more "winter blues" than usual this year and maybe the general malaise of winter found my ear latching onto the word "comfort" more eagerly than usual.

I haven't made a search of this, but I don't think there's much in the way of comfort in most Christmas hymnody (overlooking, for this post, secular Christmas music, which often has sad themes). It's usually very joyful. Some hymns may be darkened by the foreshadowing of the cross. Advent music has some comfort talk, particularly the popular hymn based upon Isaiah 40, "Comfort,

Comfort Now My People." Still, Christmas seems to be more about joy, celebration, bright angels and awe of the common folk.

Or maybe "comfort" is all over the material. Like I said, I haven't taken the time to search other hymns for this message. But this year, I heard the unspoken message behind the line, "tidings of comfort and joy," precisely that some people are discomfited, maybe even inconsolable. Much more significant than my winter blues, I can see stories of different Facebook friends losing family and friends in a myriad of ways, sometimes weekly. These deaths remind me of my own losses, and the grief can return in unexpected ways. Mind you, I have much to be happy about, too, much joy in my life. Still, the need to be comforted is never far away.

I suddenly heard "comfort and joy" as the lyrical equivalent of a shadow in a painting. Just as shading in a drawing gives dimension, the reminder that we also need comfort gives Christmas a deeper background, even as it draws our attention to other elements in the foreground.

Christmas brings a bundle of emotions, really, a bundle than even the magic of Santa couldn't get down a chimney. Along with those emotions comes

God-with-us (Immanuel), who is there through loss and gain, pain and recovery, death and resurrection.

Comfort and joy. Tidings of comfort and joy.

Good News finds you where you are.

Meet the Authors (in order of appearance):

Chloe S. Flanagan is an author, technical editor, and graduate of New York University. She enjoys exploring themes of faith, love, and radical grace in her writing. In her free time, Chloe loves listening to music, singing, traveling, reading books in all genres, and spending time with family.

Joya Polk (they/them) is a Black, queer, neurodivergent, non-binary trans person. Originally from North Carolina, they grew up in Houston, TX where they fostered their love for writing and the arts! Joya is a playwright and a poet, wrote, directed and produced 3 original plays: Making Moves (2015), Maybe Tomorrow (2016), & RESET (2018), and self-published their poetry book, "She Speaks" (2019). Their short play, "Halloween BS" was featured in the play festival, Haunted Love, organized by Sis in association with Andrew B. Feldman's Barthtober Fest (2020).

Joya now resides in Baton Rouge, LA with their partner, their two dogs and two cats, and they work as an American Sign Language interpreter while continuing to write and advocate for Black and Trans/Queer rights. Their journey can be found at @joya2theworld2 on Instagram.

Karen Eisenbrey lives in Seattle, WA, where she leads a quiet, orderly life and invents stories to make up for it. Karen writes fantasy and science fiction novels, as well as short fiction in a variety of genres and the occasional poem or song if it insists. She is the author of five novels: The Gospel According to St. Rage; Barbara and the Rage Brigade; Daughter of Magic; Wizard Girl; and Death's Midwife, all from Not A Pipe Publishing. Karen shares her life with her husband, two young adult sons, and one elderly cat.

Allison K. García is a Licensed Professional Counselor with a passion for writing. Latina at heart, Allison has absorbed the love and culture of her friends and family and has used her personal queer experiences to cast a glimpse into the journey of marginalized Christians.
bit.ly/allisonkgarciaauthor
www.facebook.com/allisonkgarciaauthor
www.instagram.com/allisonkgarciaauthor
www.twitter.com/athewriter

Ha Na Park is an ordained minister in the United Church of Canada, currently serving Immanuel United Church, in Winnipeg. She/they finds the personal faithful journey in the context of interspiritual traditions (especially East Asian religions, Christianity, and atheism.) Her/their interest extends to queer of colour critique. She/they co-organized the Queer and Faithful Conference in 2019 and is currently a member of Korean Rainbow United as the co-founder with her friends.

Meagan Ruby Wagner is a mother, wife, sister, daughter, and writer from Ohio. She loves reading and baking and walking in the woods. Her debut collection of poetry, Honeysuckle, is available on Amazon.

Henry J. Barnosky is an amateur horror writer and professional overthinker currently living in New England. After an embarrassing baptism at the age of seven, Henry was baptized "for real this time" when he was sixteen, which he takes as a heartwarming reminder that our God is the God of second chances. Now, as a gay transman in his early twenties, he hopes to be a living example to others that queer Christians can live and thrive in the face of adversity. His favorite Christmas tradition is watching Die Hard every Christmas Eve.

Ziel is a queer Christian artist from Boston, MA. They love biblically accurate angels, wild DnD sessions with dear friends, and queer community. Eventually they will have official artist pages, but if you are interested in their current chaotic creation style, you can check them out on tiktok @zielstarfallen.

Raelee May Carpenter is pan squared (a pangender pansexual who wrote their first novel at age 7 (it wasn't publishable, but they wrote it). Raelee is a member of chosen family that covers four continents and has a slight obsession with Latin Urbano music.

Avery Arden (they/them or ze/zir; formerly Avery Smith) is an autistic, genderqueer, leftist minister and author of *The Kin-dom in the Rubble,* a book of queer Christian poetry. They graduated from Louisville Presbyterian Theological Seminary with an MDiv in May 2019 and now live in Atlanta, Georgia, with their wonderful wife and two goofy cats. You can frequently find them engaged in embroidery or other crafts; infodumping about Jesus or tv shows or good books they've just read; going on walks; or digging into biblical Hebrew and Greek.

A firm believer that all binaries are meant to be broken, Avery is both Catholic and Protestant. Ze believes that Divinity thrums through all of Creation and breathes life into every human community, not just Christian ones.

Most of Avery's ministry — focusing on trans & queer, disability, and interfaith theologies — takes place online. For a full list of where you can find Avery's work, visit linktr.ee/queerlychristian. Reach out to them with inquiries or just to chat at queerlychristian36@gmail.com.

Blake Ellis Edwards is a writing tutor turned generalist academic coach. He is a trans queer Christian. When he's not espousing the importance of commas after initial dependent clauses, you can find him petting a cat, reading tarot, or playing Dragon Age: Inquisition.

SJ Blasko is a poet and fantasy writer from Boston, Massachusetts. As a disabled LGBTQ+ Christian, much of their work revolves around the intersections of mental health, chronic illness, queerness, faith, and identity. They have published three poetry collections: *Midnight Comes* (2018), *the flowers need love to grow too* (2020), and *TREE* (2021), and their next book, *Recordari*, will release in January of 2022. You can keep up with their frequent book yelling and (infrequent) posts on instagram: @thesongsofsparrow.

Neil Ellis Orts is a writer living in Houston. His creative writing has appeared in several small press journals and anthologies and his novella, Cary and John is available wherever you order books. Visit him online at neilellisorts.com

Ruckus Aquinas is a gay, neurodivergent Ex-Evangelical and instrument hoarder making art for the marginalized and vulnerable. You can find his music at www.ruckusaquinas.com

Johanna E. H. (they/she) is a poet from Charlottesville, Virginia. After dropping out of high school, she spends her days walking dogs, reading and writing, singing in a local choir, being active in queer Christian and leftist communities, and healing. You can find her at https://johannahallwrites.com.